ALSO BY RUSSELL NOHELTY

THE OBSIDIAN SPINDLE SAGA
The Sleeping Beauty
The Wicked Witch
The Fairy Queen

The Red Rider
THE GODVERSE CHRONICLES
And Death Followed Behind Her
And Doom Followed Behind Her
And Ruin Followed Behind Her
And Hell Followed Behind Her
And Conquest Followed Behind Them
And Darkness Followed Behind Her
And Chaos Followed Behind Them
Katrina Hates the Dead
Pixie Dust
OTHER NOVEL WORK
My Father Didn't Kill Himself
Sorry for Existing
Gumshoes: The Case of Madison's Father
The Invasion Saga
The Vessel
Worst Thing in the Universe
The Void Calls Us Home
The Marked Ones
OTHER ILLUSTRATED WORK
The Little Bird and the Little Worm
Ichabod Jones: Monster Hunter
Gherkin Boy
www.russellnohelty.com

BLACK JACK

Book 2 of the Wonderland duology

By:

Russell Nohelty

Edited by:

Jonas Saul

Proofread by:

Lily Luchesi

Toni Cox

Cover by:

Paramita Bhattacharjee

CHAPTER ONE

I hated myself for saying it, but being transferred to a sleepy department north of Wonderland wasn't all terrible. I thought I would miss the high-stakes life or death action of the 91st precinct, but it absolutely was not the worst thing that ever happened to me, even if it stemmed from the worst thing that ever happened to me.

My sister Dinah took my timidity in bashing everything about my new boss as a tacit agreement that she was right the whole time about me moving to the suburbs, but not hating every second of my life was a far cry from falling in love with the slower pace. Perhaps Dinah loathed her new life so deeply that she forgot enjoyment and hatred were two different emotions.

That would explain quite a lot about my sister, actually, and the constant bickering about my choices that created the din of my relationship with her.

"Are you coming to dinner tonight?" she asked as we stood in the butcher line at the H.E.B., an enormous, pristine grocery store very different from the grimy bodegas I used to frequent. She filled a whole cart and part of another (that she forced me to push) for a single week of cooking. Meanwhile, everything I ate fit in a single basket and consisted mostly of coffee and vodka, with a couple of TV dinners thrown in for good measure (and so my sister would not get on my case about eating out every meal).

"It's Friday, isn't it?" I asked. "That's the tradition."

"Well, it's a new tradition," she replied. "Usually, you had a case that prevented you from coming over, or something always came up."

I sucked my teeth. "Yeah, about half of those were complete lies."

"Only half?" she asked with a chipper smile. "I figured as much, but I'm surprised you are so forthright about it."

"Forthright is my new MO, sis."

"That's nice. I like that." She looked down at my basket disapprovingly. "Now, we just have to teach you to cook."

"I know how to cook," I replied. "That's why I don't wanna do it."

"Arthur is not going to stay with you long if you don't learn how to feed him."

Arthur was my boyfriend. He worked as a journalist, which meant he kept the same awful hours as me and didn't mind when I blew him off for a case, and I didn't mind when he had a late deadline. We met up, had our fun, and went our separate ways. It was about the only type of relationship I was capable of at the moment, and I wasn't looking to get any more serious than what we had.

Sometimes, I could tell he wanted more, but then a case would break for me, or he would get a scoop, and the tension would break. Once, we had a long enough conversation to warrant a pregnant pause, which led to a long silence. It was the kind of silence that was usually filled with professions of love or deep questions about the future, but when he opened his mouth to speak, I defused the situation by sticking my tongue in it, and all was well.

"I don't need to feed him. I just have to fuck him, and while I'm a hell of a screw-up, I am a master in the bedroom." I smirked at her. "Maybe you should try that instead of spending all day in the kitchen."

"Excuse me!" Dinah said with an exasperated scoff. "We have two kids, and I can guarantee you they didn't come from a stork."

"Sure," I replied. "But when was the last time you guys had sex?"

Dinah shrugged. "I guess it's been a while, but we're very busy, both of us."

"Sure, sure. I mean, I get it. I just wish you got it, too."

"That is a very gross wish," she replied. "Please stop wishing about my sex life."

The conversation about my sister's bedroom activities was mercifully cut short when the butcher called our number, and we placed our order. Dinah needed a pot roast to put in the crock pot before she went to work, and I had the day off, and idle hands were a devil's plaything.

Once we were finished, Dinah walked to her car, and I went to mine. She had picked up a job at a real estate office in the afternoons to keep her own idle hands busy, and I brought myself home to put my meager groceries in the fridge.

I stayed in my old place, even though the move would save thirty minutes and two subway transfers. It was part the habit, part the metal door my old department installed to prevent protesters from ripping me apart, and part because I hoped that my old department would come to their senses and bring me back to vice. Of course, that part of me wasn't stupid. You can't send twenty officers into a trap that got them killed and not expect there to be consequences.

I couldn't even go to their funerals and pay my respects. The police commissioner literally told me I would be fired and arrested if I showed up within five hundred feet of any of their families, and he wasn't messing around. Even Caterpillar couldn't bring me back into their good graces.

After putting away my groceries, I flopped onto the couch, hoping to get some sleep, but dreading it at the same time. Sleep meant dreams, and that's when the charred bodies of the narcs I led to their deaths haunted me.

I closed my eyes, but the screaming, charred zombies of my fellow officers I sent to their deaths jolted me awake. It haunted me in the quiet moments, preventing me from getting a moment's peace for many, many months. Since I couldn't sleep, I pulled out my phone and texted Arthur.

Me: Come over.

Him: Working.

Me: Now.

Him: ...

Him: I'll be right there.

Me: Damn right.

I smirked and put away my phone. You absolutely didn't have to cook for your man if you could fuck him into oblivion. If you could do that, they would answer your beck and call like a horny little puppy.

CHAPTER TWO

After Arthur was done satisfying me, he rolled off my chest and let out a deep, contented sigh. I turned to him and smiled. "So, was it worth blowing your scoop?"

He laughed. "There will be another one. Besides, these press conferences are always a bore. I'll call my buddy and get the details before the deadline."

He didn't answer my question. He was always evasive like that. He couldn't give me a simple yes or no answer, and it frustrated me to no end. "So…"

He caught my eye for a second before shaking his head. "You really are a needy dame; did you know that?"

"Rude." I scoffed and hit him with one of my pillows as I stood and walked to the bathroom. "Who says things like that? What are you, a reporter from the twenties? Do you have one of those bills in the brim of your derby?"

There was a beat of silence as he thought about it. "But dear, I literally am a reporter from the twenties."

Grr. He was right. "The 2020s was not what I meant, and you know it."

"You're a cop, Alice. You, of all people, should know the value of being precise, especially to a reporter."

I closed the door to the bathroom for some privacy. He was annoying, especially in the way he always had to be right, but it was nice to match wits with somebody again. Most of the men I slept with were barely good for three pumps and a grunt before they lost their value to me. For all the aggravation he caused, Arthur kept things interesting.

"Hey," he asked when I was finally done in the bathroom. "Why do girls always pee after sex?"

I looked at him foolishly. "Are you serious?"

"Why?" he replied, cocking his head. "Is that a stupid question?"

"Well, you're a thirty-year-old man who has been sexually active for at least a couple of months, and you're a reporter, so I figured you would know."

He shrugged. "I never really thought about it."

I walked over to the dresser to grab a new pair of underwear so I could take a shower and prepare for dinner with the family. "You ask questions about every little thing in the universe, and you never thought to ask about that?"

He furrowed his brow. "It never came up."

"You have a computer, a phone, and a database at work with thousands of experts at your disposal. Look it up."

He sat up. "Yeah, but I'm asking you."

"It's a very sexy question, my friend."

"I'm not trying to be sexy. I was just trying to have a conversation. Seriously, you think I'm frustrating? How about how you aggressively refuse to answer even the smallest question?"

"I'm not refusing to answer," I replied, taking off my shirt. "I'm just agog at the fact you don't know your dick is filled with bacteria, and if I don't pee, I'll get a UTI. I don't know if you've ever had one of them, but they aren't pleasant."

"Hrm." He seemed pensive. "That makes sense. Do you have to poop after butt stuff?"

"I'm not having this conversation." I walked back to the bathroom. "You need to go, or I'll be late for dinner."

He hopped off the bed. "When are you going to invite me to your sister's house? We've been together for a while now."

"As fuck buddies, and nothing more." I laughed. "Never. You will never, ever meet my family."

His face dropped. "Oh."

I threw my clothes on the counter and turned on the shower. "Does that upset you?"

"Well, yeah. I thought maybe this was going somewhere, but if I'm never going to meet your family, then it means—"

This was the conversation I was trying to avoid. I turned off the water because it was about to get awkward, and I didn't want to waste a month's worth of water while I had a fight with the person I was sleeping with.

"That's exactly what it means," I said. "And you know I don't want to talk about this."

"But I do. Doesn't that count for something?"

"Absolutely not. This isn't going Dutch on a pizza. You don't have that conversation just to appease the other person. It's like sex. If one person doesn't want to have it, you don't force it on them, or you're an asshole."

"So, I'm an asshole now?" There was scorn in his voice.

"Oh my god, you are such an asshole, but until this moment, the kind of asshole which was charming in their way. Now, you're just being the annoying type of asshole."

He threw on his pants. "I didn't know it was annoying to want to be around you, to want to grow closer to you."

"Have you met me?" My eyebrows furrowed. "Getting emotional is about the most annoying thing you could ever do to me, and getting close to me means sharing emotions. No, thank you."

"You're a real bitch, you know that?"

"Yes!" I shouted enthusiastically. "I am absolutely aware I'm hard to love and harder to like. I know I'm complicated and messed up, but that's who I am. If you don't like it, then you can see yourself to the door." I turned on the water again. "And if you're not okay with being around my particular brand of crazy, you don't have to come back."

"That's not—"

"If you do, though, then know this is as much as I can give. It's the most I want to give. I'm not going to change, and I don't want to change. I don't want you to stay around because you think I'll somehow mend myself together and become a whole, real person in a year or two because that's not going to happen, and you're wasting your time."

I closed the door to the bathroom and locked it behind me. I heard Arthur bang on the door as I stepped into the shower, but I wasn't about to let him in. I didn't want him to see me cry, and the shower drowned out my whimpering. I bit my lip until the noise finally stopped, and I heard him walk to the front door and slam it behind him.

Why was I like this? Arthur was a fine person who seemed to genuinely like me. The most annoying thing about him was that he wanted to spend time with me and get to know me better. That wasn't so bad, was it? Then why did it feel like being stabbed with a hot knife every time he opened his mouth?

I finished my shower and dried myself off. I didn't look at myself in the mirror much anymore, and I stopped wearing makeup completely. People always said the natural look was in, but I still got plenty of looks when I went places like I was a pasty, hot mess that could do with a pound of foundation to cover the bags under my eyes and blotchy skin.

By the time I finished dressing and getting myself ready, it was well past the time I should have left. Luckily, I had a squad car that wasn't due back until tomorrow and had no problem running lights to speed my way through the city.

My phone buzzed when I went to pick it up, and my heart dropped when I saw the text. It was from Caterpillar. I hadn't heard from him in months.

I need to see you. Get to the club. Now.

Well, I guess I'm not seeing my sister tonight after all.

CHAPTER THREE

The Looking Glass Lounge. I hadn't thought of it much since my exile from the south side of Wonderland. The day I cleared out my desk and relocated to the sleepiest precinct in the entire city, Caterpillar stopped contacting me. It was the one good thing about being forced away from the streets I loved so well. I made a deal with the devil to regain my badge, and I owed him my soul. I thought for a moment he lost interest in me, perhaps that he made a bad gamble and decided to cut his losses, but men like Caterpillar didn't forget, and they certainly didn't forgive. I didn't know what he wanted from me, but I couldn't leave him waiting. Not unless I wanted to bring down his wrath on everything and everyone I cared about.

The Looking Glass Lounge seemed different from the last time I walked through its doors. Then, it was rather inviting, if seedy, but since I last saw it, the club had been fortified with iron bars on the windows and a thick metal door which put mine to shame. There were always guards patrolling the perimeter, but now they had tripled and manned heavy machine gun turrets on every corner of the roof.

Caterpillar was going to war, and whatever words I said to him failed to dissuade him of that notion. I hoped things would have calmed down since I left him after the explosion that killed twenty of my fellow officers, but that was clearly naïve, and I wasn't one for naivete. I hadn't heard about any gang violence, and I took that to mean there wasn't any. However, I should have known better…it just meant whatever violence there was didn't make the papers. I would have to talk to Arthur about that at our next dalliance, assuming he still wanted anything to do with me after our last exchange.

I knocked on the thick metal door, and it barely made a sound through the thick rebar. I went to knock a second time, but a small slot slid open, and two bulging, bloodshot eyes glared at me.

"What do you want?"

"I'm here to see Caterpillar."

"Isn't everyone. He ain't taking vis—"

"Is that Ahlice?" Caterpillar's lyrical voice carried on the air. "Check her badge and lhet her in!"

The bouncer growled as I pulled out my badge, and then, after a long moment, the door clicked, and he let me in. Sweat and musk wafted through the door as it cracked open, and I pushed through the riveted metal door.

Gone were the dancers and the gentlemen they ground against, replaced by soldiers in heavy armor and assault rifles that populated the stages and bars. There had always been an eerie joy to the club, but that had been replaced with a silent pall, where not even music played to drown out the tension.

"Ah, there yhou are!" Caterpillar shouted from a booth behind a half dozen of the biggest monsters I had ever seen. Most of the rich morphers had transformed themselves into elegant animals, but the brutish bruisers of the world preferred bulky predators. One of the men resembled a burly black bear and another a hairy wolf, while a third transformed themselves perfectly into a walking tiger, complete with stripes marking their face and arms.

Two other men were mid-transition, one into a boar with massive tusks, and another had barely started a transformation into a Komodo dragon, with bright red eyes and scales on half their face. Then there was a regal lion who stood above them all.

They parted for me reluctantly, and I made my way up the stairs to Caterpillar's booth. He tried to maintain the elegance that once oozed out of him, but there was a tremble on his lips that belied his bravado, and he gripped a cane tightly in his hand to prevent him from shaking like a leaf.

"I see you took my warning to heart," I said. "I thought we agreed to let things die down before you formed an army."

"Yes, whell that whas back when yhou were going to handle things, and nhow, whell, yhou abandoned me, and here whe are."

"I didn't abandon you. I was reassigned. You could have stepped in and—"

He waved his hand dismissively. "I only have so mhany hands to play, and I already stepped out on a limb for yhou once. One more step and the lhimb whould have cracked. Then, where whould I be?"

"In the same place you are now, I bet, but with one more ally on your side."

He smirked. "That's cute. No, my dear. I whould have fhallen from a great height and been fhound bhloodied and broken on the ground. I like yhou, but not enough to die for yhou."

It was time to stop beating around the bush. "Then what do you want from me now? I was quite happy in my quiet little hamlet. So, if all you wanted was to chastise me, I should be going."

Caterpillar slammed his cane on the table, creating a crack that echoed throughout the club and caused all eyes to turn to us. "Yhou do not make the rhules here, Alice. Yhou still mhade a promise to me that yhou are my man until I say otherwhise. I have not said otherwhise, and thus, yhou are still mine."

"Then speak your piece, because I have other things to do today."

He snapped his fingers, and three men rushed out of the room. "Oh, I think yhour dance chard whill be quite fhull for a very long while."

The door to a back room opened, and the men dragged a beaten and bruised body into the room. When they threw it down at my feet, I recognized the mangled remains immediately.

William. The boy I brought to Caterpillar for safety after he helped me stop a gang war, and now he was dead at my feet.

CHAPTER FOUR

"What have you done?" I shouted, rushing over to William's dead body. I didn't know him well, but he helped stop an all-out gang war, and for that, I was eternally grateful to him.

"Me?" Caterpillar said, startled. "Yhou must be joking."

I had left William in Caterpillar's care after the explosion—no, that wasn't right. I abandoned him here, and when I moved uptown, I forgot about him entirely. Out of sight, out of mind, and now he was dead.

"If not you, then who?" I turned to him, my eyes straining to keep the tears from falling down my cheek.

"That is what I whant yhou to fhind out," Caterpillar said, standing. "William whas uhnder my care, and as such, untouchable by all bhut those who whish for a shwift rhetribution. This is an act of whar, and one I am vhery whilling to join once I know the culprit."

"You don't want a war," I said, standing.

"Oh, I vhery much do, but if I start a whar whithout cause, I lhose all the protections affhorded me by the police." He smiled at me. "Which is where yhou come in."

"I don't understand."

"Yhou are one of the fhew I can trust. The White Queen's fhingerprints are all over this, but she has infhiltrated every inch of the police fhorce and corrupted even my mhost trusted contacts…all except yhou. I nheed yhou to prove this whas her dhoing, and then I whill have my righteous whar."

"There's not a lot I can do. I'm a disgraced cop whom everyone hates."

"Which is why yhou are the perfhect pherson to help me. No ohne with half a braihn whould whaste their time and money on a disgraced offhicer reassigned to the bhoonies, and yhet, I have, and thus, I have an asset my enemies whould not dare corrupt."

"That is super depressing, but I can't fault your logic."

He snapped his fingers again. "Brilliant. Then yhou will invhestigate this case, and fhind out who killed my man, and when yhou do, I whill handle them."

"I'm not going to help you kill anyone," I said. "You might own me, but I won't get blood on my hands."

"Oh, my dear, but yhou already have." He shook his head. "But do not whorry, yhour name whill be kept out of any retribution, and yhou can sleep whell knowing you have stopped a gang whar."

"And if I refuse?" I asked.

"Then yhou whill have broken our agrheement, and I whill see you suffher." His eyes narrowed. "And yhour family whill fheel my whrath as whell."

My lip curled in a snarl. "If you threaten my family again, I will kill you where you stand."

Thirty guns cocked and pointed at my head before Caterpillar waved them off. "No nheed for that. She is just imphetuous." He stepped toward me. "I whould hate to resort to that. They are innocents in ahll of this. However, there are many who whill suffher if yhou do not help me, and I cannot predict where the stray bullets whill land."

"I don't like this."

He shrugged. "Yhou're not supphosed to. There ahre no good options here, Alice. Please believe I whould much rhather have a dhozen beautiful whomen dancing in this club insthead of an ahrmy of fhoul-smelling men, but whe are all making sahcrifices in this trying time. I am noht immune to them, and nheither are yhou."

I took a deep breath. It was impossible to argue with him, no matter how much I wanted to. He owned me until such time as I was released from his service, and even if he hadn't contacted me in months, that was no less true. Besides, I truly feared what he would do if I didn't help him.

"What do I have to do?" I asked.

"Why, it's as simple as it is complhicated." He swung his cane in the air. "Simply, yhou mhust do your job. Fhind the khiller and bring them to jhustice. The complhicated part is more complhicated."

"Lay it on me." The hair on my neck bristled at the thought of what he would say next. "It can't be any worse than what I've put up with the past couple of months."

"Don't be so shure," he replied. "Yhou whill be reassigned to yhour old department, which is bhetter equipphed to handle such things than the phodunk precinct yhou whork for now." He held up his hand as I tried to speak. "Don't thank me; it's alrheady been ahrranged."

"Thank you?" I asked bitterly. "Those people hate me. I led their friends into a slaughter, and I'm going to have a bullet in my back the minute I walk through the door."

"Be that as it mhay, there are several offhicers on the White Queen's phayroll, and it is my hope they can lhead yhou to the killer."

"You think the killer is a cop?" I asked.

"Stranger things have happened. Whoever khilled this poor bhoy, yhou ahre not wrong. Yhou whill whalk into the lion's den, and whill only come out ahlive if yhou ahre vhery carefhul."

"I don't like this." I bit my lip. "But I don't suppose I have much of a choice."

"Nhot unless yhou intend to rhun from me the rhest of yhour natural life."

I didn't. "Then, I guess I'll do it."

"Yhou alwhays have a choice. It just might nhot be a good ohne."

CHAPTER FIVE

My sister hadn't stopped calling and texting since I walked into the Looking Glass Lounge, and I couldn't deny her anymore when I slid back into my car.

"Jesus Christ, Alice!" Dinah shouted when I picked up the phone. "I thought you were literally dead. Do you know how to call somebody when you're going to be late?"

"I'm sorry," I said. "Something came up, and—"

"No excuses," Dinah said. "I thought you were over this bullshit, Alice. I thought we had turned a corner."

I sighed. "I thought so, too, but—well, I am what I am, Dinah, and I know that's not good enough for you, but—"

"Don't give me that sad sack bullshit, either. You promised you would be here, and then you disappeared. I was really worried about you."

"I'm sorry," I said with a sigh. "Is there any more pot roast? I'm kind of hungry."

"You are so lucky I love you. I saved you a plate."

Things were about to get very hard, and I knew starting tomorrow, there would be no time for Dinah, not until I solved Caterpillar's case and brought peace back to Wonderland.

Wow, you really are naïve, aren't you, Alice?

Peace to Wonderland? There hadn't been peace since the rule of the Red Queen, and even then, the only peace came from being high out of our minds all the time. Still, peace would be nice right now after so much strife. Was it really worth it, fighting against White Rabbit when succumbing to it was so much easier?

I wasn't too proud to admit that I succumbed to the thrall of Rabbit a few times since my reassignment. Times were tough, and Rabbit was easy. It made everything okay, if only for a moment. My hand twitched as I drove to Dinah's house just thinking about it. She would never understand why I needed Rabbit, just a little bump to drift off to bed. I hadn't had a good night's sleep since killing that poor boy, and Rabbit took the edge off; it allowed me to sleep and dream pleasant things like flamingos playing tennis and otters drinking tea.

Life wasn't the kind of thing Dinah wanted to avoid. She got everything she wanted. I thought I did, too, but the longer I fell down the rabbit hole of my own existence, the less I was sure I knew what I wanted or wanted what I had. Dinah would say I could never be satisfied, but I didn't think it was that; not really. I thought I wanted what I had when I was young and naïve. I didn't know what it meant to make the choices I did, and now that I had everything I ever wanted, it made me wonder if I knew then what I knew now, would I have been willing to make the same sacrifices?

I didn't have to think of anything like that with Rabbit. I just had to think about what silly hat I would wear to the otter's tea party, and that was enough.

When I finally rang the doorbell to Dinah's house, she answered it with a yawn. "It's about time."

"Sorry, were you in bed?"

"It's eight-thirty; of course, I was asleep."

"Sounds terrible," I replied, but I wasn't sure I believed it. I would be up until the wee hours of the morning, trying to fall asleep without Rabbit and failing before I finally succumbed to the thrall of it. Was that better than sleeping at a normal hour?

"Well, come in then."

She shuffled me into the house. There was a steaming plate of pot roast, along with some mashed potatoes and vegetable medley, on the table. I sat down and started to eat voraciously, stopping every few bites only to tell her how much I enjoyed the food or how sorry I was to blow her off.

It wasn't until I was finally done that she slid back in her chair, and the smile left her face. "So, do you want to talk about it?"

I placed my fork on the table. "Not especially. It's the same old bullshit, come at me in a different form, but I'll get through it."

"I don't want you to get through it," Dinah replied, her brow furrowing. "I want you to thrive for once. I thought you were finally doing that, but now I see that old look on your face like everything is about to fall apart if you don't hold tight enough to prevent it from happening."

"We all have our lots in life, Dinah, and this is mine."

"It doesn't have to be. You don't have kids, or a husband, or anything tying you down. You could go to Denver tonight, or Los Angeles, or any stupid place and start over."

I smiled at her. "That does sound nice, but I am a stubborn old mule, and I'm set in my ways."

"Your ways suck, then."

"I know, but they are mine." I stood up. "I wanted to come by and say thank you for all you've done for me for the last few weeks. I'm really appreciative of it."

Her eyes narrowed. "You sound like you're going off to war."

"Something like that, and I don't think I'll be coming around a lot for a while." Tears welled in her eyes as I spoke. "But when all this is over, I hope we can do this again."

"It's never going to be over, is it?"

"No." I sighed. "I don't suppose it will be, but that is my lot in life. I gotta hold those sticks tightly so they don't fall apart on me."

"That's stupid," Dinah said, bitterness on her breath.

"It is, but it's my stupid, and we all have our lots in life. This is mine." I walked to the door. "Night, Dinah. Tell the family I sent my love. I hope I see you on the other side."

CHAPTER SIX

When I got back home later that night, Arthur was waiting for me, sleeping with his head curled up in his knees. I had no idea how long he waited there, but when I checked my phone, he hadn't reached out since our exchange earlier.

"You realize this is one of the worst neighborhoods in Wonderland, right?" I asked. "I'm surprised you didn't get shanked."

It really wasn't all that bad, but I was trying to make a point. Besides, even in the worst neighborhoods, people didn't go around shanking people for the hell of it.

"You're home," he groaned when his sleepy eyes opened.

"What are you doing here, Arthur? And why didn't you call?"

He rubbed his eyes. "I thought I would surprise you, and then I figured you wouldn't be long, so I decided to wait."

"That's weird," I replied, handing him the papers. "You understand how weird that is, right?"

He yawned. "I'm used to sleeping in weird places, Alice. I can fall asleep just about anywhere."

I found that to be true in my experience. Arthur had a habit of nodding off in movie theaters, at dinner, and even, once, on a Ferris wheel. I thought he had narcolepsy for a long time, but he assured me that he simply pushed his body to the limit until he couldn't fight sleep anymore, even through the coffee and Adderall he popped to keep him lucid.

"Well, come in then," I said, unlocking my door and walking inside. "This doesn't make up for our fight, you know. I'm still pissed about that."

"You're pissed?" He scoffed. "I'm the one who was rebuffed."

I growled at him. "I've told you a dozen times I don't want to have a relationship, yet you keep forcing the issue. It's annoying as fuck."

"Yeah, well, I keep thinking you'll change your mind."

I felt my blood pressure spiking, so I raised my hands in the air. "I don't want to fight about this tonight. If you came to argue, I'd kindly ask you to leave."

He smirked. "And if I don't."

My eyes narrowed. "Then I will beat the fuck out of you."

His tone changed to one of soothing excitement. "I might like that."

Arthur was a bit of a masochist and liked when I yelled at him. It was one of the reasons we got along so well. I was a bit of a bitch, and he enjoyed it, even through his consternation. In fact, I often thought he provoked me so he could get aroused.

"I'm not in the mood for this, Arthur," I said sternly.

He wrapped his hands around me. "Not in the mood for what? We're just talking."

"I know that tone." I couldn't deny that his touch sent tingles up my spine, and I let out a sigh as he lifted my shirt to wrap his arms around my stomach. "You're playing a dangerous game."

I tilted my head to give Arthur access to the nape of my neck, a cue which he took with gusto, wrapping his lips around my bare skin and sending a jolt of excitement through me. I hadn't met a man who made my body ache for him since Dormouse. He took me with force and vigor, twisting me to his selfish aims, and I thought that was how I wanted to be fucked, but Arthur caressed every inch of me like he was building a map to the most intimate crevices of my body.

Dormouse took me violently and passionately, and when it was over, he tossed me aside like a used condom, but Arthur relished every bit of my body, spending long moments on places I didn't know could make me stir with passion, and he didn't thrust himself inside me until I was aching for him with every inch of my body, and then even longer.

He adored my moaning, writhing body against him as I clawed at his hair and pulled him from my thighs up to my mouth, tasting myself on his tongue as he pressed his lips tightly to mine, and I sucked every breath from his throat.

It wasn't until I nearly begged for it that he finally gave me every inch of himself, over and over again, as I wrapped my legs around his and pulled him closer to me with every thrust of his dick inside of me. I never came for anyone like I did for him, and even after two, three, four orgasms, he kept giving me more and more of himself until he quivered in ecstasy, and his sweaty body fell onto mine.

When he finally rolled off me, I remembered for a fleeting moment the reason I threw him out of my house earlier that day, but then it floated out of my mind like so many other fights over the last few weeks.

"Can I stay over?" he asked as he pulled his underwear over his naked butt. "Or will you kick me out into the cold?"

"You can sleep here," I replied. "It's the least I can do, but if you bring up a relationship again, I'm going to brain you."

"Fair enough," he said, disappearing into the bathroom. "I guess I can live with that."

CHAPTER SEVEN

I couldn't sleep even in the best of circumstances, but with Arthur's incessant snoring, it was particularly impossible now. He also liked to wrap his burly arm around me while he slept, which had a habit of tickling my nose and making me uncomfortably hot, yet pushing him off of me only lasted a few minutes until he returned, like a heat-seeking cuddle monster.

The only recourse was to slide off the bed and escape to the couch, where I could get some privacy. There were many reasons not to get into a relationship with Arthur, not the least of which was that he hogged the bed, and when confronted about it, he simply apologized but said there was nothing he could do because it was all in his sleep.

Selfish awake, selfish asleep, only not selfish when he took me to bed, and since that was ninety percent of what I cared about when taking a lover, it worked fine for me, as long as he didn't get closer than that.

I turned on the television, keeping it low so Arthur remained asleep. I didn't know why I tried to be polite to him. He slept like a grizzly bear in the middle of winter, after all. I cycled between the channels and scrolled through Netflix, but there was nothing that caught my eye. Even those British baking shows didn't catch my fancy, and I could usually stare mindlessly at them for hours.

It wasn't until I finally turned off the television and sat in silence that I realized the reason why I couldn't find anything to satiate me. Many Rabbit junkies talked of an "itch" so powerful they could think of nothing else. Mine wasn't nearly as prevalent as all that. It mostly presented itself as an antsy nervousness, a restlessness that prevented me from finding any solace in the dark of night.

I stood and walked to the small dresser near the window, out of place against the rest of the furniture in the living room, and opened a small drawer at the top usually reserved for brushes and hair ties. In the back of the drawer was a small black case that housed an opal ring to anyone nosy enough to snoop through my personals. However, buried under the velvet stand were what remained of two pills given to me by a hog-faced dealer in the aftermath of the horrible mistake that saw me transferred from my old job into the doldrums of the northern city.

I had learned over the past year that, while snorting a full capsule of Rabbit could easily get you killed or hooked so deeply on the stuff that you might as well be dead, a microdose of the stuff was enough to take the edge off a really shitty day. Yes, over time, that might lead to an addiction, but I was smart enough to stop before it ever got that bad. After all, it was kind of my job. I knew the signs. All I had to do was be careful.

They had used microdosing of LSD for years to treat psychiatric problems to great effect and didn't create a bunch of junkies, and while the city council prevented any experimentation on White Rabbit under penalty of death, I was quite sure it would have a similar effect as LSD or magic mushrooms for that manner.

I had finished one of the pills and only had three-fourths of the second one remaining. I pulled out a nail file and shaved off enough of the remaining pill to make a small pile on the dresser. I stashed the pill away and made the pile into a small line. I took a deep breath and closed one nostril before sniffing the line into my nose. When it was done, I took what remained and gnashed it on my teeth, then I sat back and waited for the high to kick in.

The effects of Rabbit came slowly and then all at once. The walls turned from a dull gray to a bright, vivid pink over the course of five minutes, and then in a flash, everything began to meld into the Wonderland I had visited several times over the last few months.

I stood on shaky legs and hobbled to the door. When I went to turn it, the doorknob came to life and let out a loud squeak. I giggled to myself for a full minute before heading out into the night, careful to pat my new friend on the head as thanks for letting me out of the door without incident.

By the time I reached the bottom of the stairs, the rest of the White Rabbit had taken effect. Instead of the drab streets common to my neighborhood, everywhere I stepped was lined with hyper-saturated flowers that sang and hummed as I walked, and the streets were populated with all manner of incredible creatures.

I knew better than to wave at them or initiate conversation, for they were likely not in the same drug-addled haze as I was at the moment, and interacting with the population of Wonderland even in the best of circumstances wasn't advised, so despite my buoyant mood, I kept my smile tight on my lips, and my hands firmly thrust inside my pockets.

I stopped in at the shawarma restaurant on the corner to find the owner had turned into a large pickle with a long face and warts all over his body.

"What can I get you, Alice?" he said in a sing-songy way.

I pointed at the hunk of meat behind his head that had grown its own arms and legs and asked for a gyro. The man cut hunks of meat off the spit and handed it to me. The first time I ordered one of them, I thought the poor spit would scream out in pain, but it was more than happy to give pieces of itself away, and the pieces of meat sang happy songs as I swallowed them down.

After having a meal, I watched as the streetlights danced on their corners and listened to the bricks outside my building tell stories about the good old days. However, soon enough, my alarm rang, and I headed back inside. A small dose of White Rabbit only lasted for half an hour, and then you crashed so hard it was impossible to drag yourself back to your house.

I realized that the first time I wandered too far and ended up asleep in an alley. My feet felt heavy when I brought them up the stairs, and by the time I shut the door and said goodnight to the doorknob, my head dragged on the ground, my arms behind it.

I barely made it back to the couch when the walls turned back to an ugly, muddy gray, and my eyes grew so heavy I could no longer keep them open.

CHAPTER EIGHT

I woke up with a vicious hangover. My throat was dry, and my head pounded as I made my way shakily to the kitchen. I downed a glass of water and four aspirin before starting a pot of coffee.

Arthur wasn't in bed, and he didn't have the courtesy to make it, either. I didn't hear him in the shower, which meant he must have left somewhere in the night. All the better because the last thing I wanted to do was speak with him again.

My solitude was short-lived as I heard the door open, and Arthur stepped inside carrying a paper bag. He smiled widely when he saw me. "Good morning. You slept like the dead last night. Didn't even hear me leave to get bagels."

He didn't apologize for forcing me off my own bed. "I'm not hungry."

"Are you sure?" He slid out a sandwich stuffed with lox and cream cheese on an everything bagel. "I know it's your favorite."

I growled as I snatched the bagel and took a big bite of it. He was right. This was my absolute favorite breakfast and objectively the best breakfast in the world. I would fight anyone who said otherwise.

"Are you really not going to say anything about kicking me out of my own bed last night?" I asked after swallowing a big bite.

"What do you think the bagels are for? It's my way of apologizing."

I looked down at the bagel. "It's a good start, but I still want to hear it for once. Next time I'm sending you home."

"I can sleep on the couch," he replied, taking a tiny bite of his own sandwich.

"How is that any different than going home?" I asked.

"Then I don't have to drag my ass out in the cold and drive halfway across town," he replied. "Since you refuse to come to my place, I think that's a pretty good compromise."

"I don't refuse. It's just never convenient."

"Oh, I know how deeply inconvenient it is," he replied, his mouth full of food. "I come down from the east side to this shitty hole enough."

"You don't have to come over. But if you want to fuck me, then you'll do it on my terms, or not at all."

"How romantic." His voice filled with exasperation.

"It's not supposed to be romantic. That's not what I want, and it's not what I'm willing to give. The absolute last thing I want is romance."

"Again, something I know. I never met a girl who would rather have a cheap breakfast over a nice meal."

I held up the lox bagel. "This is not a cheap sandwich. I don't think anything is cheap in Wonderland, but this is not cheap anywhere."

"Cheaper than a meal at Chez Paris."

"And better. I hate that place." I took another bite of my sandwich and let silence fill in the air for a long moment. "Hey, why aren't you guys reporting on the gang war between Caterpillar and the White Queen?"

It was something that had weighed on my mind since talking with Caterpillar, and there wasn't a better way to wedge it into a conversation aside from doing so uncomfortably.

"That's not up to me, it's up to the assignment editor, and they don't think there's a story there."

I chuckled. "You don't think there's a story in the fact that somebody is trying to muscle in on the biggest dealer of Rabbit in the city?"

"Caterpillar has gone out of his way to ensure nobody ties him to the White Rabbit trade, and the White Queen is little more than a myth. Do you have any idea what would happen if we printed something like that? We'd have half the city in chaos and a lawsuit on our hands from the biggest 'not a drug dealer' in Wonderland."

"A myth?" I said. "She blew up a house and killed twenty police officers, along with a bunch of other people."

"Allegedly, but there's been nothing solid to corroborate that. Without hard evidence, I can't just print anything I want. That's libel, and I'll be sued."

"If the White Queen comes out of the woodwork to sue you, then I will pay your legal fees."

"You don't have the money." He smiled at me, cream cheese on his face. "I'm working on exposing the war, though. That's what I've been working on the past few weeks in every spare hour I'm not with you."

"And why didn't you tell me?"

"Not like there's a lot of time to talk between fucking and sleeping," he said, wiping cream cheese from his mouth. "Besides, I didn't want to upset you. I know how much being tossed out of your old precinct hurt you, and half of my best sources are narcs you would recognize."

"I don't think that's going to be a problem anymore." I put my sandwich down. "I got reassigned back there to handle a case."

"That's great."

I smiled. "You don't know the case. It's anything but great, but I appreciate your enthusiasm. I only wish I had half of your excitement."

He walked over and kissed me on the forehead. "Then I'll be excited for both of us."

I leaned my head against his chest. "Don't think this changes anything between us."

"I won't."

I held out my hand. "And I'll take my key back now, please."

He sighed, thinking he might have pulled one over on me. "Fine. What's to make you think I didn't make a duplicate?"

I kissed him on the cheek as I gripped it in my hand. "Because you know if you did, then I would kill you on the spot. Besides, if you had a key, why would you be lying on the floor in front of my door?"

"Maybe I'm just waiting for the right moment to use it."

I raised my eyebrow. "Now you have me worried. Do you have a key to my place?"

He stopped for a second before smiling. "Of course not. I'm not a psychopath."

"That is yet to be confirmed."

CHAPTER NINE

In the last bit of humiliation of my old new life, I had to deliver my squad car back to my old station and take the train back downtown to the 91st precinct. I felt the cold eyes of judgment from every single person that wandered through my train car. I thought myself crazy thinking complete strangers were judging me before I remembered it wasn't long ago my face was plastered across every front page and nightly news segment in Wonderland. Up in the northern part of the city, they gave you the courtesy of whispering behind your back when you were out of earshot, but in the mean streets of south Wonderland, they stabbed you right in the front, out in the open.

I used to think it was a blessing that people in my neighborhood wore their hearts on their sleeves, but one of the things I appreciated about polite society was that they did you the courtesy of letting you live your life without feeling like a pariah every second of every day. The officers I worked with gave me sideways glances in my first days there, but once they found that I was quiet and kept to myself, they did the same. They might have hated me as vehemently as my old cohorts in the 91st precinct, but they let me live in blissful ignorance of that fact.

The subway jerked to a stop at Clifford Street, and I wandered out of the ancient subway car littered with graffiti, another thing I once found charming but now found horrid upon further inspection. How could a police force that let every inch of their city be defaced protect anyone? Maybe that was the point, after all, nobody was safe on my old beat; some were luckier than others.

Even in the worst neighborhood, most people were going to live. Even in the days of the Bubonic Plague, half of Europe lived. It was a horrible tragedy, but you had a coin-flip chance of surviving, and the same was true in even the worst streets in Wonderland. Only so many people could be riddled with bullets every day, and you were probably going to survive, until you didn't.

I heard the sounds of the police station before I even finished walking up the stairs. The sounds of sirens blared out of the parking lot next to the station. There was an antiseptic smell that permeated the street around the station, and it was cleaner than any of the buildings around it. That's not because they cleaned it more often than other places, though that might certainly be part of it. No, it was because people kept their distance from the entrance to the station in all but the most dire circumstances. The police were not to be trusted unless absolutely necessary, and even then, proceed with extreme caution, like a rabid dog you found on the street.

Two black-suited officers pulled an unfortunate sap up the stairs to the police station, paying me no mind. The last time I came to the station, everyone paid me mind. It was after the explosion that killed twenty officers and sent me to the boonies. Before then, reporters swarmed me for weeks when I tried to enter the building. Maybe it was for the best that they sent me away. I didn't want to be a distraction, but a prickle running up my spine said that was exactly what I was about to be.

The entrance in the parking garage opened up to the uniformed officer's bullpen, but the front entrance brought you right into processing. Drunks, junkies, and every manner of miscreant sat handcuffed on the benches in front of a long hallway as overworked and underpaid clerks processed them into the jail deep underneath us; the same jail where a young boy had been murdered in my last days on the job down here.

"Liddell!" Aman's voice boomed over the bullpen where dozens of plainclothes detectives worked on cases big and small, and sometimes small ones that broke into something big. Aman looked like he had lost some weight since I last saw him, but he was just as disheveled as our last encounter, where he sent me away. "Get back here!"

I walked slowly through the bullpen, skirting around the tight desks that littered the cramped area. Well, if looks could kill, I would have been dead a dozen times over from my fellow officers by the time I got back to Aman's office.

I was used to being stared at like a pariah down in the basement, but the plainclothes detectives had the common courtesy to glare to wound, not kill.

Dormouse hung up on a call as I neared his desk. He was still a strapping specimen of a man, but gone was the warmth he once had for me. He hadn't tried to reach out once since I was reassigned, and none of my many messages were returned until, eventually, I got the message that he wanted nothing to do with me either.

"Hi," I said, waving at him, but he simply confirmed my suspicions by turning to his computer and pretending to busy himself with shuffling files on his desk. I bit my lip to avoid the pain of rejection and turned my attention to Aman, who gave me the biggest death glare of them all.

"You got a lot of nerve showing yourself here."

"I didn—"

"Don't talk," he growled, his jaw clenched. "Just get inside before you cause a riot."

"Yes, sir," I said, ducking into his office as the door slammed closed behind me.

CHAPTER TEN

"This wasn't my idea," I said before I could even sit down, and when I saw the fury Aman brought to bear on his desk, I thought better of taking a seat and instead held back against the far wall.

"Don't give me that bullshit. You have been trying to get back here since I kicked you out, and your friend Caterpillar finally made it happen."

My eyes narrowed. "Are you fucking crazy? I admit I kind of hated you when I left, and for a while, I was bitter about it, but you couldn't pay me to come back to this place"—I pointed out the window to the rows of eyes looking into the room through the slatted curtains—"and those motherfuckers waiting for me to mess up so they can draw and quarter me. Are you out of your damned mind?"

"Don't raise your voice at me, Alice." His voice was more measured than it was previously, but it still held all the ire and heat that he felt toward me.

"I'm not a child, Aman. If you yell at me, I'm going to come right back at you because I absolutely don't give a fuck. I don't want to be here any more than you want me here, but we're stuck with each other."

He eyed me up and down for a long moment. "You really didn't call in any favors?"

"What favors do I have to call in with Caterpillar, huh? In case you forgot, I got twenty of his people killed. He probably hates me worse than you do."

"I highly doubt that."

"I made him look weak, and you can't make powerful people look weak. They don't take kindly to that. I feel like there's a sword of Damocles over my head, waiting for me to fuck up so he can finally be done with me."

I didn't realize it was true until the words escaped my lips, but the more I thought about it, the more I believed it. Caterpillar didn't send me back here to be his mole. He sent me back here because he knew somebody would take care of me for him, and it was only a matter of time before the problem of Alice was a distant memory, and in that memory, whatever plan he concocted for the better me, he hoped to get when he bargained for my soul could be brought to fruition.

"Are you still loyal to him?" Aman asked, staring deep into my eyes as if a deep truth could be seen in them.

"Fuck off if you have to ask that," I spat at him. "I wouldn't be here if I wasn't."

"Sorry," he replied. "But I have to ask. You have no idea how many people have abandoned him for the White Queen in the past couple of months. Since—well, you know."

I shook my head. "No, I can guess, but how about you tell me?"

He bit his lip. "After the explosion, nobody felt safe with Caterpillar anymore, but I kept the peace, for the most part. I told them that the White Queen wasn't a friend to the police. Anyone who could kill narcs like that—she's nobody I want to be in business with … but then, the payouts came. Double, triple what Caterpillar paid even his top men, more than he paid me."

"And they defected?"

"Some of them outright, and others were cagey about it." He looked out the window toward the bullpen, and everyone watching turned back to their work. "I still don't know everyone who switched their loyalties, who's playing both sides against the middle, and who remained loyal to Caterpillar." He turned to me. "I guess that's why you're here."

I nodded. "Nobody would bother with a washed-up, washed-out cop. Hell, she might have used my loyalty to Caterpillar as a cudgel to turn some of those that hate me most."

He chuckled. "I wouldn't put it past her."

"Any idea who she is?" I asked.

"Not even an inkling," he said. "Those that work for her are tightlipped, and even those whose mouths can be pried open have only met a figurehead, and even when we can track them down, turns out they never met the White Queen, either."

"Any idea what she wants?"

Aman nodded. "What they all want. Power. But until now, Caterpillar's kept the underworld under his thumb. Seems like that's no longer the case, and the White Queen is out to show she is the new baddest bitch in town."

"Which is why I'm here," I said, barely able to say it with a straight face.

"It would seem that way." He reached into his desk and pulled out a manila folder. "Caterpillar thinks finding this poor bastard's killer will lead us to her, or something like that. I tried to tell him he was just some punk kid caught in the middle of a drug war, but apparently the kid was working on something for him, and it got him killed."

"Sounds familiar."

He tossed the file to me. "I'd tell you to be careful, but I really don't give a shit whether you live or die."

"Always the charmer." I grabbed the manila folder. "Any other bad news?"

"Yeah, actually." He chuckled. "I'm pairing you with Dormouse for this one since he's the only detective who doesn't actively want to kill you."

"You sure about that?" I asked. "That's not the impression I got."

"Either way…" Aman started before trailing off. "He's the only one I know won't pull the trigger."

"You have more faith in him than me."

Aman looked up at me. "He worked with you a long time and never put a bullet in your head, and I don't think you would have lived that long with anyone else, and that's before you killed twenty of their friends."

"I would prefer to work alone."

"Tough shit. I hate him nearly as much as I hate you. So far as I'm concerned, if you make each other miserable, I'm killing two birds with one stone. Now, get out of here before you make me vomit up my lunch at the sight of you."

I placed my hand on the doorknob. "Seriously, Captain, you could teach lessons on wooing a girl. My heart is all aflutter."

CHAPTER ELEVEN

The absolute last person I wanted to have a conversation with was Dormouse … no, that wasn't true. The absolute last person I wanted to have a conversation with was the wife or husband of any of the good officers I had a hand in killing in that explosion, but by the way Dormouse looked at me as I approached, he wasn't far behind.

"We should talk," I said, sidling up to him.

"Nothing to talk about," he replied.

"Are you kidding me? We watched twenty men blow up, and then you watched me take all the punishment for—"

He rose in his chair and grabbed my arm so tight I thought he might rip it off. "Not here."

He didn't say anything again until we were out the door and around the side alley of the building. Luckily, none of the smoking crew were on a break, so we had at least a merciful few minutes by ourselves.

"Talk," he growled.

I looked at him for a long moment, barely able to contain the anger boiling inside me. For months I stayed silent as he ignored me, as the guilt festered for what I did, but looking at him now, completely unfazed by an event that ruined my life, made me madder than I thought possible.

"You … you son of a—" My hand balled into a fist, and before I could stop it, my arm shot up, and I decked Dormouse in the face. He stumbled backward several feet before standing straight and rubbing his cheek. "I'm not even going to apologize."

"Why would you apologize for anything?" He massaged his jaw. "This is all a big joke to you."

"Are you fucking serious right now? I reached out a dozen times, more than that, trying to bridge the gap between us—to see if you were okay—and now I find out not only are you okay, but you're acting like nothing happened."

"Oh, something happened. Something absolutely happened, and it's all because I defended you."

"Great, so I'm the cause of all your problems? That sounds familiar."

"We would never have been there that night if it wasn't for you!" he screamed, lunging forward like an out-of-control behemoth. "So yes, I do blame you for everything!"

"That's complete horseshit!" I screamed back, standing my ground as he moved closer to me. "We solved that case together. We both put the pieces together, and we were both to blame!"

No!" he shouted. "You pushed—" He was crying now. "You always push. We should have gotten a warrant and followed the chain of command, but instead, you called the captain and used…"

"Used what?" I asked.

"How long were you working for Caterpillar?" His voice was lower, and it felt as if he had no energy left.

"I… I…" I didn't expect such a bold question.

"I should have known." He rubbed his hands against his glistening bald head. "How else could you get back on the force without—does it feel good, knowing that calling in a favor to your boss got twenty good men killed? Do you have any idea the shitstorm that fell on all our heads while you were basking in the lap of luxury in—"

"Lap of luxury? They sent me to the boonies to live the most boring life possib—"

"No," Dormouse replied. "Caterpillar protected you—protected himself."

My eyes narrowed. "What are you talking about? Aman told me Caterpillar couldn't protect me, and that was why I was being sent away."

"I don't know the details, but they wanted to bring you in, arrest you, arrest both of us. Instead, I got a slap on the wrist, and you got a new assignment. I guess they couldn't have a trial dragging out all the corruption on the force."

Suddenly, it connected for me. "That's what she was after all along."

"What?" Dormouse said. "I'm talking about Cate—"

"Not him." I paced across the alley. "The White Queen was trying to get us arrested, so we could be put on trial. She knew everything would come out if we took the stand." I turned to him. "Do you know what this means?"

"I have to admit, I'm barely paying attention."

"Shit," I said. "I was hoping you would know what that meant."

"Sorry to disappoint you, but I have no idea. She already has connections in city hall, the prosecutor's office, and nearly every precinct—"

"Except for the 23rd," I replied. "I'll bet that was why they sent me there because it would be away from the White Queen's reach."

Dormouse looked up at me. "Then why bring you back here now?"

"I don't know." I held up the manila folder. "But it has something to do with this case, I can feel it. I know you hate me, and I'm not too fond of you, but we worked together for a long time. You're the only person I trust in this world, and I don't even trust you much right now. We have to solve this case if you want me out of your hair."

"You're like herpes, Alice. You never leave. You just go into remission. The only way to get rid of you is for one of us to die."

"That is a morbid thought," I replied. "But I have no intention of dying any time soon."

"A pity."

I growled. "Fine, I'll do it on my own."

I turned to leave, then felt a yank on my arm. When I turned back, Dormouse was looking at me and holding out his free hand. "Wait, I can't let you do this alone, as much as I'm sure Charlotte would love for me to let you fail. Give me the case file. Let's catch the bastard who killed that poor kid."

I placed the folder in his hand. "That's the first intelligent thing you've said all day."

CHAPTER TWELVE

Caterpillar used William's body for show, and after he made his point with me, he called Aman to conveniently "find" the body and bring it to the lab, which was where it rested, waiting for us to examine it. Dormouse led us back through the precinct and into the elevator after our spat, where he pushed the button for the sub-basement. I knew the way just as well as him, but this was his house and no longer mine, so I let him lead, happy to follow for the moment. Those that led had a habit of getting the first bullet, and in a hostile environment, you wanted to hide as much as possible from incoming threats.

The morgue wasn't a place most detectives liked, but I didn't have too much of a problem with it. The smell could turn a stomach and cause more than a few NARCOs to wretch into a trash can, but I had a stomach of steel, and Dormouse's was made of iron. Still, neither of us particularly liked the look of dead bodies, which was why we both worked vice instead of homicide.

"I wondered when I might see you two," Dr. Gerald said as he looked up from the blonde teenager he had splayed open on his table, examining their insides. "Welcome back, Detective Liddell. I hope they are treating you well."

He wasn't having a piss, but every word out of Dr. Gerald's mouth oozed with the kind of sarcasm that would have gotten better men punched in the face, but that was just his way. He wasn't particularly social or well-liked, and we bonded over the fact that we were the two most hated people in the whole department. It was no surprise that he welcomed me back with open arms because, without me, he was the pariah of the department. With me close, at least he could shield himself behind the scalding hatred everyone had for me.

"It's good to see you, Doctor," I replied.

"You don't have to lie about it," he said with a sly grin that showed too much of his teeth for comfort and too little lip. "Let me finish up here, and I'll bring our boy out of cold storage."

We waited a few minutes for him to prepare the body for the freezer behind him, and then watched as he wheeled the poor, dead woman to one of the boxes and slid her inside. "Don't worry about her anymore. She was young, but she died of natural causes. An embolism in her head. I envy her."

"That's morbid, Doc," Dormouse said. He didn't find the same charm in the awkward man as I did, and I could see it only just underneath many layers of creepy.

"Oh really?" The doctor turned toward us. "After all you've been through, can you truly say you don't envy the dead? They have no concerns, no fears, and no pain. They don't have to worry about being caught by their wives screwing their partners or the fallout of that partner shooting a child."

"Watch yourself, Doctor," Dormouse growled. I couldn't blame him for his anger one bit.

"Oh, I'm sorry," he replied with the same creepy grin. "I didn't know it was some big secret. I hear things down here, including many things people wish I didn't. The dead tell no tales, but they have their secrets."

"Can we just see the body?" I said, trying to diffuse the situation and the ramblings of a socially awkward man before he got laid out on the ground. "Please."

"Of course." He walked to the other side of the room and pulled out another body from his wall filled with them. "Will you help me for a moment, Detective? I can't quite get the leverage to lift this body on my own."

Dormouse walked over cautiously as if the doctor was a leper who could transmit his particular peculiarities to him if he got too close. Together, they pulled the body down and wheeled him on a stretcher over to the center of the room.

"I already finished my examination, but I thought you would like the full show on your big return to our little domain."

"I really don't, but he's right here, so how about you just get on with it."

"Of course," he replied with a deep bow. "He was strangled with a piano wire, or something of the like, not unlike that boy who died in our cells in the last months of your first stint with us, Detective Liddell." He moved his hands up to the neck and pointed at a deep gash. "Unlike that poor fellow, though, there was a struggle beforehand, and he had several bruises pre-mortem. Unfortunately, there was no salvageable DNA on them or the fingernails."

"Do you have anything that can help us?" I asked.

"Well, all data is helpful, is it not?" He cocked his head as if the idea that his ramblings weren't helpful was absurd. "I can tell you the attacker was bigger than him and wore a gray, tweed blazer. Odd, since that fashion is almost exclusively used by professors."

"That's slightly more helpful," Dormouse replied.

"There is one other thing that came up in my investigation." He walked over to his computer and reached into a bag next to it. "I examined the contents of the stomach and found this."

I leaned closer to see a playing card, but not just any playing card—*a Black Jack.*

CHAPTER THIRTEEN

Black Jack was the new pseudonym for Jack Fowler, a brutal enforcer for the Red Queen. While he was on the queen's payroll, they called him by another name: *Suicide.*

After the Red Queen went to jail and the Cards were disbanded, many found work as mercenaries or hired guns for companies and powerful people. Jack decided he could make a quick buck lending his services to the rich elites of Wonderland. After a string of successful jobs, he founded a company to help his fellow Cards find employment. His company quickly grew, and Black Jack became one of the biggest security companies in Wonderland.

There was a saying among the NARCOs: half of the Cards went into illegal crime, and the other half worked for Black Jack and did crime legally. It wasn't a great saying, but it was accurate. All the Cards were dirty; it was just a matter of how dirty they were willing to get. Black Jack had no problem calling in his criminal buddies if the need arose.

His calling card was a playing card, rather obvious if you ask me, of a Suicide Jack stabbing himself in the head. Usually, it's a suicide king in most traditional card decks, but Black Jack had one commissioned specifically for him. He liked to say that if you didn't hire him, it was like stabbing yourself in the head, but I knew the real reason they called him "suicide." It was because he would take jobs nobody else was dumb enough or crazy enough to do. The type that was sure to get you killed, except somehow Jack always survived. He had a bit of a reputation as a hothead, but even a bigger one for taking on jobs everyone else turned down and turning them into successes. That's how he made his bones post-Wonderland, and his company became synonymous with taking on any job, no matter how dangerous or how illegal.

Every NARCO in Wonderland knew they were dirty, but since most of us were on the take, too, we couldn't do anything but hold up our noses and let them wallow in the stink with us.

Black Jack didn't take a side in the White Rabbit trade, except to stay clear of it. Jack wasn't a smart man, but he knew better than to side against Caterpillar, or at least I thought he did until I saw William's body. The card William swallowed told a different story, and if Black Jack took sides against Caterpillar, it likely meant he was working with the White Queen, and it was the first real lead we had in tracking her down. The one thing Black Jack insisted on was meeting his clients face to face, which meant if he were working with her, he would have seen her face.

Of course, these were assumptions. It was just as likely somebody planted the card and forced it down William's throat to implicate Black Jack in the crime. Everyone who was anyone in the criminal underworld knew Black Jack always left his calling card at the scene of his crimes for the Red Queen. It was the legend that made him famous.

After finishing with Dr. Gerald, I took the card across the hallway to the forensics department and gave it to N'baka for analysis.

"I must admit," N'baka said after looking at it, "I've always heard about these cards but never seen one in the flesh."

"Count yourself lucky. You don't want to be on Suicide's bad side."

"Suicide?" N'baka asked. "You mean Black Jack?"

"Right. Of course."

When I first joined the force, my training partner and I landed a case that involved Black Jack, and he told me everything. Roi was an old, grizzled cop before I met him, and he went back to the old days, before the fall of the Red Queen. He was a low-level Card himself, one of the few that went "legit" and stayed off Black Jack's payroll. He told me stories of working with Suicide and how crazy he could be if forced into a corner. Luckily, the case took us another way, but I met him twice, and he was a bear of a man—and not the cute kind. No, he was the type that had been shot four times and still found a way to survive, the kind that fought wolves for sport and wore the scars with pride.

It would take a couple of hours to get the results back from the test, and I had to get out of the precinct before the stench of hatred became too much to take, so I decided to head across town and meet Arthur for a late lunch. I had a habit of forgetting to eat on the job, so when he texted me to see if I wanted food, I thought I could kill two birds with one stone; fill my belly, and ask him what he knew about Black Jack.

"Not more than anyone else," he said after we ordered our pastrami sandwiches. "Far as I know, he's kept his nose clean for the past few years since that row with city council."

I cocked my head. "What row?"

"Oh, right." He chuckled. "They paid a lot of money to keep it out of the papers and off the public record, but twenty years ago, right before Councilwoman Lane wrested power away from the Lories, she and Jack had a big fight. "

"I never heard about any of this."

"You really don't know who you work with, do you? Aren't you the one who told me everyone's on the take?"

"Dick." I punched him playfully in the arm as the deli counter called our number. "Tell me about the incident then since you're so informed on everything."

"Not everything." He took a bite of his sandwich. "But people do tend to like me, which makes one of us. Damn, this is good."

"Right! I'm surprised you've never been here before, given the hours you keep."

"I have failed myself," he said. "I guess I needed a cool woman to bring me here."

"Flattery will get you nowhere. Now, about the incident."

He thought for a moment, savoring every bite of his sandwich. "They had a fight on an elevator that led to a bunch of lawsuits. She accused him of threatening her and sexual harassment, and he countersued for defamation."

"Jack Fowler threatened the head of the council?"

"She wasn't that then. This was before the last election, before she took power back from the Lories."

"How did they resolve it?"

"In the dead of night, there was a settlement, sealed by the courts, and it all went away. After that, she won the election in stunning fashion."

"That part I remember," I said. "It's the other part I'm fuzzy on."

"Well, it was quite a few years ago at this point. I had barely graduated college."

The phone buzzed, and I saw a text from Dormouse. *Text results inconclusive. Meet me @ Black Jack. Let's rattle a cage.*

I wolfed down the rest of my sandwich and wiped my mouth. "I need to go."

"Lovely company as always."

I stood up. "Flattery will get you nowhere."

He looked up at me. "Can I see you tonight?"

"I'll see how I feel after this meeting."

"Fingers crossed it's good news."

"Frankly, I don't know what will be good news at this point. Whatever gets me out of that station quicker, I guess."

"Then I hope for that."

"Me too."

CHAPTER FOURTEEN

There was no point telling Caterpillar any of this yet. It would only cause him undue stress, and in the worst of situations, he would jump to a conclusion that would not be conducive to the investigation. He only wanted me to tell him where to point his gun so he could pull the trigger, and if I mentioned Black Jack, it would ignite a powder keg that could bring all of Wonderland down with it.

No, I would keep this information to myself and Dormouse until such time as we actually had a solid lead, a definitive person who could be blamed for the incident, and then he could take them out quickly and cleanly.

My gods. Listen to me. Acquiescing to the idea that Caterpillar was going to murder whoever was responsible for killing William without due process or a fair trial would have sent me into a moral quandary even a few months ago, but now it was like water rolling off my back, and even that idea didn't affect me much, except for pointing out that it should have affected me more.

Black Jack Security occupied a high floor in a large building in the center of the Gillman District, the financial heart of Wonderland, where most of the large banks and stockbrokers had offices, and the wealthy often congregated for drinks. It was the perfect place for a security company, as every one of the scumbags working there was the worst kind of criminal, and they all needed protection. I felt sympathy for the poor in Wonderland, especially those forced into crime for their circumstances, but I had no sympathy for the rich that pushed money around and hoarded it like dragons who laughed as the rest of the city burned around them. They could have done something, anything, to help the less fortunate and improve conditions around them, but instead, they paid off politicians to let them keep their money, and paid thugs to protect them from other ultra-wealthy elites that could pat them on the back for their gaudy houses and huge portfolios.

The minute we walked into the building, surrounded by thousand-dollar suits and ten-thousand-dollar watches, the receptionists behind the glass desk at the center of the room stared at us like we were the worst kind of scum in the world. As we worked our way to them, they let out an audible gasp.

"We need to see Black Jack Security," Dormouse said.

"Do you have an appointment?" A coquettish blonde said from behind their desk.

I pulled out my badge and slammed it on the table, causing a small crack in the perfect desk. "Will this do?"

The other woman sneered at me and pulled up a phone. She spoke into it, apologized profusely, and then hung up. She looked at me with a smile that couldn't contain her disgust and pointed to the elevators behind her. "Thirtieth floor. Have a nice day."

I heard the women snicker behind us as we walked forward, but I didn't mind their jeers. If those types of people hated me, I was doing all right for myself. It was only when they treated me well that I needed to worry about my priorities.

The glass elevator doors closed, and I watched Wonderland fall away behind us as we rose higher into the air.

"That was good back there," Dormouse said. "I would have paid money to get a freeze-frame of that woman's look of shock when you showed your badge."

I shrugged. "We did have fun once."

"Too many lifetimes ago," he said with a sad sigh. "Let's not come on too strong, okay? Let's poke the beehive, not swat it down."

"No promises, but I'll do what I can to keep it under control."

Maybe he was right, but I was willing to try to capture it again, however hard it might be to do so. It didn't seem like he was of the same mindset, which was a shame, but maybe for the best. Having a wall between us kept things professional, at least.

The door opened to the thirtieth floor, and I had a hard time believing a security company worked inside. The same expensive suits and perfectly polished shoes walked through the halls. The only thing that gave it away was the sign behind the black-haired receptionist that read "Black Jack Security" with a one-eyed jack winking at us.

"Welcome," she said with a fake smile. "How can we help you?"

"We need to see Jack Fowler about a case, ma'am," Dormouse said, containing his own form of disgust. "Is he around?"

"I'm afraid Mr. Fowler is in Monaco this week, but if you need to speak with somebody, then you should talk to our head of security, Mr. Deedum. He's in a meeting now, but if you'd like to wait, he'll be with you when he has a moment."

"I think he has a moment now. I don't know if you have any idea how this works, but we're the narcs. When we come calling, you answer immediately. You don't leave us waiting."

"Well, he's in with the commissioner right now," she said, stone-faced. "And unless I'm mistaken, police commissioner ranks higher than detective. Isn't that right? Or am I as stupid as your tone makes it seem?"

Dormouse sneered, ready to lay into her until I pushed him back. "I'm sorry for my partner. I'm sure we can wait for them to be done, as long as it won't be long. After all, I'm sure Mr. Deedum doesn't want the commissioner to know your company is the focus of a criminal investigation."

"No, I don't suppose he does."

CHAPTER FIFTEEN

We waited for nearly half an hour before the door next to the receptionist opened, and a salt-and-pepper man walked out dressed in a black uniform adorned with dozens of metals and other pieces of bling. Even regular citizens that had no attachment to the NARCOs knew Commissioner Inman. He was a legend on the force, making his bones in the days after the fall of the Red Queen when things were at their most chaotic.

He was barely out of his training pants when he took down the largest bust of White Rabbit in NARCO history and rode that success to becoming the youngest captain on the force, followed by the youngest police chief and then the youngest commissioner in our city's history. He talked a good game, but the thing officers loved most about him was that he followed through with absolutely nothing except that which would get him on the evening news. He benefited from the fact that nobody else wanted his job, and those who did mysteriously disappeared. He was in bed with every criminal organization in the city and somehow kept them all in check without having them step on each other's toes.

In that way, both Dormouse and I were thorns in his side, and when he saw us, his face dropped. "Detectives. I didn't expect to see you here."

I shot up from my chair. "Or I you, Commissioner."

He looked back at the open door where a grizzled middle-aged man with a five o'clock shadow and dark, soulless black eyes stood in a suit, tailor-made to show off his broad shoulders and enormous pecs.

"Go easy on him, Detectives," the commissioner said, nodding to us. "I'll see you next month, Timothy."

"Look forward to it, sir," he replied in a gruff, but affectionate voice that did not carry over when he turned to us. "Come in, I suppose."

He led us through a maze of offices where dispatchers and office staff worked on computers and filed papers. The area was awash with chatter, which he ignored until we reached his corner office at the end of a long hallway. The room must have been soundproofed because the chatter died when he shut the door.

"How can I be of service to the NARCOs?" He put on a small smile. "Can I buy tickets to your silent auction? Or would you rather I buy pies for your bake sale?"

I pulled out a picture of William, bloody and bruised on the ground, dead. "Do you recognize this man?"

"All business, huh?" He let out a sigh. "Give it here."

"He was found yesterday evening," Dormouse added.

Mr. Deedum looked closely at the picture before shaking his head. He barely reacted to the mangled corpse. "I can't make anything out in this picture. His face is so beaten and bloody I can only make out the most basic features."

"He was found with a Black Jack in his stomach." My tone was flat. "That's the same logo as your company, isn't it? A suicide jack?"

Mr. Deedum laughed. "Are you accusing me of a crime because some poor kid swallowed a playing card? Because that is about the flimsiest excuse to harass me I've ever heard, and I've heard them all."

"We're not accusing you of anything, Mr. Deedum," Dormouse said. "We're following leads, and unfortunately, our lead led us here. We don't want to be here any more than you want us here, I guarantee you that."

"Well, that's where you're wrong. You get a nice view and some of the finest people this fair city has to offer, and I all get is you. One of us got the better end of this deal."

I wanted to punch him right then and there, but years on the force taught me how to deal with everyone in a calm and collected way until such time as they proved uncooperative. I truly wished he would prove uncooperative soon so I could slam his head into the polished oak desk where he rested his hands.

"Did you have any of your security guards stationed near the Looking Glass Lounge last night?" I asked him as monotonous as possible. I didn't know Mr. Deedum from Adam, but he didn't rise to become the head of security by chance, so I had to assume he was good at his job, including reading cues.

"Was that where the incident took place?" he asked.

I ran my tongue around the inside of my mouth, watching him for any signs of breaking. There were none. "Just answer the question."

"We have close to five hundred guards at any one time stationed all around the city. It's impossible for me to know where they are at any one time."

"You have GPS, though, don't you?" Dormouse asked. "You might not know off the top of your head, but you could find out for us, couldn't you? You wouldn't want to impede an investigation, after all."

"Of course, I wouldn't," he said. "I'll have my girls pull up the records right now. Anything else?"

Dormouse started to stand as I walked forward.

"Just one more thing. Did you work here twenty years ago, right before the Roses won the majority on the city council for the first time since the coup?"

He nodded. "I was a young buck, but I was there."

"What do you know about an incident between Councilwoman Lane and Black Jack security?"

His eyes narrowed. "I know enough to know you shouldn't know anything about that, little lady. That's far above your pay grade."

"Most things are," I replied, stepping closer. "But that doesn't answer my question."

He folded his arms across his chest. He had a tattoo of two cards, the ace of spades and the jack of spades, on his left hand. "I don't have the authority to tell you anything, but you come back with a warrant, and I'll give you everything you want." He walked behind his desk. "In fact, now that I think about it, why don't you come back with a warrant for anything you want from us? Until then, can you see yourself out, or will you need to be escorted?"

I snarled at him. "We can see ourselves out."

"Fantastic." He waved us away. "Don't let the door hit you where your maker split you."

CHAPTER SIXTEEN

Dormouse kept his mouth shut as we walked through the cubicles, and by the time we reached the elevator and the door closed behind us, his face was so red I was concerned he might not be breathing.

"You okay?" I asked.

"Of course, I'm not okay!" he screamed, throwing his hands in the air. "You blew it! What the hell was all that bullshit about twenty years ago?"

"I thought it might be relevant." I kept my tone calm because the last thing somebody needed when they were blowing up was somebody else egging them on to get even more heated. I had been in that situation with Dormouse before, and there wasn't an easy exit from a descending glass elevator. "You never know where a case is going to take you."

"I know it's not going to take me back twenty years ago!" He shouted, spinning as if to exit before thinking better of it. "This was a mistake."

"We didn't have an option. We have to work togeth—"

"No." He stuck his hand in my face. "We have to be partners, but we don't have to work together." The elevator door opened, and he rushed out. "Find your own way home."

"We literally came here separately!" I walked toward the front door as the girls at reception giggled at us. "Putz."

I guess I'm getting that search warrant by myself. No bother. I didn't mind city hall that much, despite my public failure last time I was there, or the fact that I yelled at

Councilwoman Lane's public relations person the last time I saw her for setting me up on a photoshoot with the mother of that poor boy I shot to death.

At least it wasn't the precinct. And that was the energy I used to march myself right past the lories and roses into the county clerk's office to file for a warrant to get what I needed from Black Jack Security. The evidence was flimsy at best. Hell, it was non-existent save for the contents of the dead man's stomach, but there was little else I could do besides hope we found a judge who didn't care about that kind of thing.

After all, they were rampant in Wonderland. If a judge wasn't on Caterpillar's payroll or one of the many gangs in the city, they were probably close with the commissioner, who had a way of greasing the wheels of government so they moved smoothly and swiftly.

"This all looks in order," one of the clerks, Zhao, told me when I submitted the file. "Don't go far, Judge Philbert is light today, and I'll try to expedite this for you."

I didn't mind the wait. At least it gave me something to do and Dormouse a chance to calm down, but I didn't know many people in city hall. I didn't want to visit the jailhouse downstairs, even if it was staffed with NARCOs— especially since it was staffed with NARCOs. The only person I knew well that worked in the courthouse was Charlotte, and there was no way she wanted to see me. If I even showed up a hundred feet from her, Dormouse would hear about it, and that would lead to another level of shit that I did not want to shovel.

I sat for a while outside the clerk's office but quickly grew bored. There was one thing I could do to while away the minutes. I didn't get anywhere asking about twenty years ago at Black Jack Security, but there were two sides to that story, and the other one just happened to work down the hall.

Councilwoman Lane once said she was on my side, but that was before my actions led to the death of twenty officers. It was hard to believe anyone was on my side now, especially somebody as image-conscious as the councilwoman.

Let's hope she doesn't kick me out of her office for having the audacity to stop by.

CHAPTER SEVENTEEN

I heard Poppy's grating voice before I pushed open the thick wooden door to Councilwoman Lane's office. My back tensed, and my fists formed into balls when she turned to me. I hadn't seen her since the malt shop where I met Grace, and I had no interest in seeing her ever again. Unfortunately, as I learned all too often recently, fate had a way of throwing the people you never cared to see unavoidably right in front of your face.

"My, my my. If it isn't Detective Liddell? I thought you vanished off the face of the Earth, girl!" Her voice was bubbly, and her outfit a vivid flavor of pink that would stand out even in the most vivacious room. "It's like I've seen a ghost. How have you been?"

I fought my lip from sneering at her. "Oh, you know. Getting along any way I know how."

"Don't be so modest." She turned to a woman with a perfectly cut bob and big glasses. "We have a celebrity with us, Janet. This woman nearly brought the whole of the 91st precinct down on her head, and look at her, walking in here like nothing happened."

"That was months ago, Poppy." My hand twitched, ready to deck her, but I fought the urge with everything in my body. "I've been reassigned since then to a new precinct and happy to report no mass deaths on my watch."

She scratched her head. "That's the 23^{rd,} right? I don't think they have enough officers to warrant a mass death, even if you fucked up as bad as you did at your last job."

My face twitched, and I lunged forward on instinct. Poppy leaped back, and I caught myself before I choked the bitch out. "You talk a good game, Poppy. That is your job, after all, but out there in the streets, you need more than a pretty mouth and nice words to get things done, and sometimes, things get messy. I don't expect people like you to understand that mistakes are a part of the job. No, you might not understand mistakes, but you're more than happy to capitalize on them, as long as it deflects blame from whatever scandal you're trying to cover up that day."

She straightened herself up from the crouched position she fell into when she thought I was going to hit her and brushed her pretty pink dress clean. "How dare you come into my house and insult me? It's not my fault you are the most wretched excuse for an officer I've ever come across. And to think, I once pitied you."

"That's where we differ, Poppy. I still pity you."

"Pfft," she scoffed. "And what could you possibly pity about me? I am practically perfect in every way."

"That," I growled at her. "Because one day, that perfect veneer will pop, and you'll fall into the muck with the rest of us. It's going to kill you, Poppy."

"Is…is that a threat?" she stuttered.

I shook my head. "No, not a threat, just a prediction. I've gotten very good at wallowing in the muck. I know what I am. I've looked deep into the darkness and see nothing but the abyss staring back at me, but you? You think this world is fair and just. You think that you'll always be this pretty young thing that can't do anything wrong, but life has a way of wearing you down and revealing the truth."

"What truth?" She shook her head like I was insane.

"That it entropies to chaos, and it will take every pretty young thing and drag it through the muck, just like it did me." I chuckled at her. "You know, once I was like you, wide-eyed and idealistic. I thought my shit didn't stink, and I would change the world, but the world doesn't change, Poppy. You do. Little by little, life takes from you and takes from you until you are just as cruel and corrupt as the things you used to hate. It's going to happen to you, Poppy, and while I don't wish my fate on anyone, I will relish it when it happens to you."

"I—I think you should leave," Poppy said.

"I'm not here to see you, Poppy." I turned to the other woman. "Janet, is it?"

She nodded. "Y-y-yes."

"Don't worry, little girl. I'm not here to hurt you. I just need to see the councilwoman."

Poppy sneered. "You must be kidding. You think you can just waltz in here without an appointment, insult me, and talk to the councilwoman like it was nothing?"

I pulled out my badge. "I'm here on official business."

"That's rich," Poppy said as Janet failed to get a word in edgewise. "She doesn't work for you, and she doesn't have to answer your questions. If anything, you work for her."

I stood up straighter. "I work for the people of Wonderland, and they demand answers. Now, let me in to see her or I'll huff, puff, and blow the door down."

"She's not in!" Janet shouted as she squeezed her eyes tightly closed, trying to push me out of the room with her will. "She's in chambers until four-thirty, and then she has a dinner."

I turned to Janet. "Is that true, Janet? If I came over and looked at her schedule myself, is that what it would say?"

"Are you calling her a liar?" Poppy asked. "Because if—"

"Not her, but she looks new, and I'll bet you taught her well, so I'll ask again—"

"She's in chambers." Janet turned the monitor around to show me her schedule, and it was true. She has session until four-thirty and then a fundraising gala later that night. "See?"

"Good girl. Don't let her corrupt you." I turned to Poppy. "Tell her to call me when she has a minute."

"I will do no such thing," she replied.

"Then, I'll have to barge in here when it's very inconvenient, and I'll make sure the press is there to get a good picture of it. How long do you think it will take you to bury that one?"

"I'll make sure she gets the message," Janet said. "Now, can you please leave?"

My phone buzzed with a text message from the clerk. *The judge is ready for you.*

"Yes, it looks like I must be going." I smiled my fakest smile at Poppy. "Always a pleasure to see you."

CHAPTER EIGHTEEN

Zhao looked at me funny the minute I walked back into the clerk's office. "I'm sorry. I tried to move it around, but you pulled Judge Xi."

Judge Xi was one of the few judges that wasn't buddy-buddy with the commissioner and tended to favor defendants more than prosecutors. Judge Talbott or Singh were more compassionate to the police and golfed with Commissioner Inman every Thursday, while the rest of the circuit was in the pocket of either Caterpillar or one of the other gangs of Wonderland. Aside from Judge Fredrickson, who was bought and paid for by the Cards gang and thus would be sympathetic to their friends at Black Jack Security, there wasn't a worse judge to be in front of than Judge Xi.

I had walked twenty feet toward the door to the judge's chambers when Mr. Deedum walked through the door dressed in the fine, shiny suit he wore earlier in the day, along with a fresh shoeshine and a purple pocket square.

"We keep running into each other, don't we?" he said with a broad smile like he was the wolf who ate the chicken as he strolled up to me. He straightened his tie, revealing the tattoo on his hand. "Funny how that works."

"Too much of a coincidence to be anything but planned," I replied. "What are you doing here?"

"Oh, Judge Xi's kid goes to the same school as my boy, and we have gotten chummy over the years." Oh great. Something else I didn't know until now. "When he saw my name on his docket, he gave me a friendly call and asked me to stop by."

"I'm surprised you didn't send your lawyer. I'm sure you have a dozen on retainer."

He pulled the door open to the chambers. "That's no way to treat a friend, is it?"

Awesome, now they were friends. The hallway to the judge's chambers was done up with elaborate polished wooden walls, with big paintings of all the sturdy and hearty old judges that had ruled over thousands of cases since the fall of the Red Queen. They seemed to follow me as I passed, and I averted my eyes to avoid their creepy gaze.

Judge Xi's office was in the middle of the hallway, and when we reached the door, Mr. Deedum waved me forward. "After you."

"A gentleman. I would never have guessed that."

I knocked on the door and heard a bluster from the other side. "Come in."

I opened the door into the judge's office, which was equally ornate as the hallway. I hadn't ever seen so much wood in one place in my whole life, from the paneling on the near side of the room to the high bookcases filled with leather-bound books and even the floor, which had been polished so shiny I could see myself in it.

Judge Xi sat behind his wooden desk, shoveling a salad into his face. He finished his bite and pushed it to the side, where it rested next to one of many fat manila folders piled high all over his desk. He wiped his mouth with a napkin tucked into his collar and pulled it out before walking over to us.

"Timothy!" he shouted. "So nice to see you. How is little Charles doing these days?"

"Not so little anymore, Huazhong. He's almost as big as I am, and I hear your boy is growing up to be a fine man."

They shook hands with gusto, all smiles. "We're trying. He studies hard, but he's falling behind in history."

"Well, nobody worth anything did well in history, Huazhong. He's strong in math and science, which is what matters."

"Too right you are." He pointed to two polished wooden chairs in front of his desk. "Please sit."

"Hi," I said, walking to the far seat. "I'm Detective Liddell."

"Of course you are." His voice fell, and all the charm dropped out of it. "I've read your petition and I must say it's one of the weakest cases I've ever heard in all my years on the bench."

I rubbed my neck. "I don't think it was all that bad."

"You don't?" His eyes narrowed. "I hoped you were trying to pull one over on me and weren't as bad a cop as the reputation that preceded you. It says here that you want to subpoena his records and interview his staff because you found a half-digested playing card in the victim's stomach?"

"Not just any card, a suicide jack. They don't even make them. They were specifically made for Black Jack Security."

Judge Xi leaned back in his chair. "And you have no evidence connecting anyone at Black Jack Security to the scene of the crime?"

"Yes, we do. The card. And if we can get into his records, we would be able to—"

"Enough." He held up his hand. "I am aware of the NARCOs' desire to use city hall as their own personal rubber stamp, but I'm not so easily swayed as to simply say yes because you asked, Detective. Black Jack Security has a whole lot of sensitive information on many important members of Wonderland, and they have a sterling reputation in the community."

I stifled a laugh. "Sterling is one way to describe them. Corrupt is another."

"I think you should be a little more careful with your accusations there, pot."

"And I'm the kettle here? Very clever," I replied before turning to the judge. "If you were always going to deny my application, then why did you bring me here? Why did you bring Mr. Deedum here?"

"So you can apologize to him."

This time I did laugh. "Excuse me? I'm not some schoolgirl who threw a rock at lunch. I'm a detective, following leads wherever they take me, and this lead led me right to him."

"Really, Huazhong, this is unnecessary," Mr. Deedum said. "I do appreciate it, though. I wouldn't want to embarrass Detective Liddell any further, though I must admit this has been too delicious for words."

Judge Xi looked at me for a long, uncomfortable moment. "You are a better man than I, Timothy, but I respect your decision. I am sorry to have pulled you away from your busy schedule."

"Please," Mr. Deedum said. "I am happy to see any old friend. How about I take you out to lunch? That salad looks absolutely dreadful."

"It really is."

"Can I go then?" I said, standing. "Because I have criminals to track down."

"Go with care, Detective. Be warned, though, if you bring this kind of garbage into my courtroom again, I'll see you stripped of your badge."

"Better men than you have tried," I said under my breath, walking to the door.

"What was that?" Judge Xi said.

"Nothing, sir. I said I will take it under advisement. Have a nice lunch. I hope you don't choke on your food."

CHAPTER NINETEEN

Judge Xi was on the take, of that I was sure, and Mr. Deedum was there to pull the strings and make sure I twisted in the wind. He probably knew I would go right to city hall and had the papers shuffled to make sure that he got his preferred judge on the case.

"Hey," I said to Zhao when I exited the judge's chambers, filled with piss and vinegar. "I thought Judge Philbert was light today. Why did we get Judge Xi?"

"I don't know," Zhao replied, her eyes darting all over the place like she was lying. "I just file the paperwork, Alice. I don't—"

"Don't give me that bullshit. We both know you could've given me a different judge that would have been more beneficial to my warrants. Why did I get Judge Xi?"

"I told you, there was no way for me to—"

I slammed my hands on the table. "Stop lying to me. How much did they pay you?"

Zhao's eyes shot straight at me. "You can't—please, don't get me in trouble."

She was right. I was making a scene. "I'm going to find you after work tonight, and you're going to tell me everything."

"No—" she started, but I was already gone. It was cute that Zhao thought she had a say in whether I found her or not. Black Jack Security might be a big scary company, but I wrestled murderers and drug dealers to the ground for fun. If Mr. Deedum thought I would just go away, he had another thing coming. He had powerful friends, but I had some of my own.

I didn't want to involve Caterpillar, I really didn't, but I had a gut feeling Black Jack was hiding something, and it drove me mad that I couldn't get the information I needed through legitimate means. If Caterpillar could use me to be at his beck and call, then I could use him to get the information I needed, especially since it was for his benefit.

Still, as I pulled up to the Looking Glass Lounge, I wondered what would happen when I told Caterpillar I suspected Black Jack of killing William, but another part of me was so pissed at the son of a bitch who just fucked me and gloated about it, I almost wanted them to burn Jack's firm to the ground, consequences be damned.

There were two guards at the door, big fellas who transformed into a lion and a bull elk, respectively. I wondered how the latter could fit inside a door with four-foot antlers but decided it was best not to ask questions.

"Aliiiice," Caterpillar moaned from his spot in front of the stage. There were fewer guards than last time, and a pasty woman in metal underwear jingled herself for his pleasure against one of the poles, writhing against it like her life depended on it, and it just might have for all I knew. "Please thell me yhou have good news."

"Unfortunately, not yet, but I think I have a lead. I hesitate to tell you, though, as I don't want you to go psycho on them."

Caterpillar smiled so broadly, he looked every bit the psychopath I described him as a moment before. "That's nhot nhice, Aliiice. Do I lhook like a psychopath to yhou?"

"Stop smiling like that if you want me to answer honestly."

He grinned even broader until the smile pushed against the edges of his face. "Yhou alwhays were a charmer." He dropped his smile. "Vhery whell. I promise not to go psycho on these people. Who ahre they?"

"You can't have your people go psycho on them either."

"Drats." He snapped his fingers. "Yhou got me there."

"Promise."

"Vhery whell. The suspense is khilling me."

"We found a playing card inside the victim."

He shrugged. "So what? The Cards are a nothorious gang in Whonderland. He could have swallowed it for any number of reasons. Lhord khnows I've had stranger things in my bohody."

"It was a Black Jack…a suicide jack."

This got his attention. "Like the ohne Jack Fowler had chommissioned?"

I nodded. "Exactly like that one."

"Whell, that is considerably mhore interesting." He leaned forward. "Ahnd yhou think they had something to do whith poor Whilliam's mhurder?"

"I don't know," I replied. "But they are hiding something. I just got back from the courthouse, and they blocked a warrant request."

"Whe ahll have secrets, Alice. Some mhore than others, and Black Jack Security is among the most secretive in ahll the lhand."

I was sick of his bullshit, but all I could do was smile at him since he currently owned me. "I need to know what they know. Can you help me or not?"

"That's tricky. Pitting one disciple of the Red Queen aghainst another. What whill yhou come up whith next?"

"Do you think he gives a shit about the Red Queen? Black Jack is all about money. If you gave them enough money to break into prison and kill the Red Queen while all of Wonderland watched, they would do it."

He slid back in his chair. "That's an interhesting proposition. I'll bhet they whould succeed, too. Oh, I whould very much lhike to see that."

I pinched the bridge of my nose. "Help or not? I'm not here for games, Caterpillar."

"Whell, that's not true. You're here for anything I whant." He stood up. "If I whanted yhou to ghet down on yhour knees and suck mhy cock, you whould only say 'fhor how lhong,' because I own yhou."

"You can try it, and I'll rip your dick off." I looked up on the stage. "I know you're desperate for a lay, but there are some things I just won't do, including you."

He touched my nose with the tip of his finger, and I bit at it when he pulled it away. "Yhou're no fhun."

"I've heard that before. Now, for the third time, are you going to help me or not?"

He rubbed his chin. "I happen to have in my employ several people who can help yhou."

"Wonderful."

"They ahre unsavory characters." He grinned at me as he pulled a notepad from his pocket and wrote a note. "Yhou dhon't have a problem whith that, dho yhou?"

"I came to you for help, didn't I?"

He ripped the paper and handed it to me. "Tell Dodo I shent yhou, and they whon't hurt yhou…much."

CHAPTER TWENTY

The note Caterpillar gave me had an address and '8pm' underlined three times, which gave me enough time to return home and get a quick shower. I needed it after the stench of Black Jack Security, Dormouse, Aman, and Caterpillar swirled around to create a sickly smell on all my clothing.

"There you are!" Dinah shouted as I rounded the corner to my apartment. "Where have you been? I've been worried sick."

"At work," I replied. "And why are you worried?"

"I've been texting you all day, and you haven't answered."

I looked at my phone but didn't see anything. "There are no texts. I've had my phone all day. I would have felt it, but I got nothing from you."

She looked down at her phone. "No, no. Not texted. I Facebook messaged you."

"I haven't looked at Facebook for months." I opened the app to see a dozen messages from her, each more desperate than the last until the last one said *I'm coming over*. "Yup. There they are. I thought we talked about this."

"We did, but I was talking to Rita, and I must have just…" She sighed. "You're okay, though, which is the most important thing."

I glanced up to see the time. "Don't you have to pick up the kids soon?"

"No, it's okay. Josh has them for the afternoon."

"Babysitting?" I asked.

"No." She looked at me in disgust. "They're his children. He's not babysitting. He's parenting."

I held up my hands. "Okay, you are in rare form. Come upstairs and have a drink to calm your nerves."

"Before driving home? That's smart."

I pressed my fingers against my temple. "Gods give me strength. Then go if you want, but I'm fine. You don't have to worry anymore."

"I will always worry while you live in this horrible neighborhood. I don't know why you won't move to Sedonus. It's closer to work."

"There's no subway, and I will blow my brains out." I walked past her toward the front door. "If you're not coming up, then I'll see you later."

"Well…" She looked consternated for a moment. "I guess one drink won't kill me."

"That's the spirit."

My apartment was a third-floor walkup, and by the top of the first landing, Dinah was winded. She had kids to take care of, but even with the constant movement, suburban life made her soft. We stopped between each flight until we got to my floor, and my heart plummeted.

My door was open. I rushed forward to see the lock had been smashed in, and everything inside had been ransacked. "What the hell—"

"What happened here?" Dinah asked.

"I have no idea. I mean, I have a lot of enemies."

"Yeah, that much I know about you. Everyone seems to want a piece, but who would actually take action?"

I didn't know. I thought I was safe inside my apartment. Even in the height of the protests against me, nobody dared smash through my room, even in the heat of anger. I walked back to the door to see the jamb had been smashed in, which knocked the door loose. I thought they designed this to withstand a blow like that, though. I thought there were safeguards in place.

I brought my hand to my mouth as I realized I had been living in a death trap all these months. Every time I thought I was safe, I wasn't. No, I was as exposed as ever, and only by the grace of the gods, I survived. I could have been killed at any point.

I stayed in my apartment because of that stupid door, and now I knew it was worthless. Every time I could have spent more hours with my family or avoided the brutal subway ride back to the south side, and it was all for naught. I was just deluding myself to think I was safe. Worse, now whoever broke in had some incriminating evidence on me.

"I'll start inventorying everything. You call the police."

"Yeah, right," I replied. "For all I know, the police are the ones that did this."

But it didn't take me long to realize that wasn't the case because as I walked to the bathroom, I came across a playing card.

A black suicide jack, staring up at me from the ground and smiling. *Those fuckers.*

CHAPTER TWENTY-ONE

I wanted to storm Black Jack Security, but Dinah convinced me to wait for the professionals like a responsible adult. When the police finally arrived, I remembered a feeling I hadn't had since my father died, and they informed me he would never be coming home again. It was a feeling of helplessness, and anger, righteous anger, swirling inside my stomach, building on itself as the police officer grilled me with questions.

"And you weren't home at the time of the incident?"

"You know I wasn't, Eduardo," I growled back at him. Of course, my apartment was in the jurisdiction of the 91st precinct, so they sent a pair of officers to case the place and take witness statements, and of course, I knew them. Eduardo Diaz and Colin Hunt weren't the two worst officers on the force, and they were new enough that they didn't hate me quite as much as some of their peers, but the general vibe definitely washed off on them, and they relished treating me like an incompetent damsel in distress.

"Don't get snippy with me. It's not my fault somebody entered your house and ransacked it…or is this how you always leave it, Liddell?"

"Watch it, kid," I whispered to him. "I've been doing this since before you were born."

"Yes, I know you're old." He looked around the room. His partner had already left after rummaging through my underwear drawer for far too long. "I guess I have everything I need here, ma'am."

Officer Diaz left, and I turned to Dinah, who was shaking her head in disbelief. "What dicks. Is that how they always treat you?"

"No," I replied, watching him turn the corner. "They're usually way worse."

"Wow. Remind me why you want to work there so much?"

"Honestly, I'm not even sure anymore."

In the silence between our words, Dormouse rushed into the door. "Jesus Christ, Liddell. What happened here?"

"Somebody broke in and rummaged through my stuff." I walked to the counter and handed him the Black Jack card on it. "Either Mr. Deedum is the ballsiest person in the world, or somebody wants us to believe they came into my place and ransacked it."

"I've met that son of a bitch," he replied, "and I honestly don't know which one to believe."

"Me either. Luckily, I have a lead on somebody who can help me figure out if it's him or not."

Dormouse gave me a look that was somewhere between "and why wasn't I invited" and "did Caterpillar help you with that" before he turned back to the card. "What about the Cards? Could they be making a play against Black Jack?"

"That doesn't sound like their MO. They are petty criminals and thugs, not masterminds." It took me a moment to connect with Dinah's eyes and realize she was still there. "Oh right. You're here."

She had her arms wrapped around herself. "Yeah, I wanted to make sure you were all right, but it seems like you have everything under control now. Do you need a place to sleep tonight?"

"Maybe," I replied, thinking of Arthur. "I have a friend who would kill to have me sleep over, but I'm not sure if I can handle that right now."

"I'll leave the key—"

"I know." She always left the key in a hide-a-key rock she poorly hid under a shrub next to her front door. "Thank you."

She gave me a kiss on the cheek and then hurried out of the room. Dormouse waited a minute before he spoke. "New beau?"

"I wouldn't call him that, but he's been begging me to stay with him for a long time. Maybe this is a sign from the universe that I should take him up on his offer." We had fallen into new patterns so fast I almost forgot he screamed at me the last time we spoke. "Are we going to talk about you being a huge dick at Black Jack earlier today?"

"I don't know if I would say huge dick."

"You screamed at me like I was a four-year-old and then stormed out. I was going to say a massive dick, but then I thought I would give you a little credit."

Dormouse bit his lip. "This has been really hard on Charlotte and the kids. When she found out you had been assigned back to me, she went apoplectic and walked out on me. It was the last in a long line of shit I'd eaten in the past few months. You have no idea how hard this has been for me."

"No, I don't, but you could have told me." I touched his arm. "I thought we were friends."

He looked up at me. "I don't know what we are, but I don't think we could ever be friends again."

I smiled at him. "I'll settle for partners if you promise not to scream at me again."

"You know that's a promise I can't make, but I will try to stop being such a huge dick to you."

"Well, you would be the first in the 91st, and I would appreciate it." I pulled my hand back. "And seriously, once this case is done, I'm out. I don't want any part of that department anymore."

"And what if Caterpillar forces you?"

"Then I'll fucking kill him." We both laughed at that, then I stuck out my hand. "Partners?"

"Partners." He shook my hand. "But I'm not going to get involved in any of the illegal shit you're planning."

"Fair," I replied. "Then it looks like you're on stakeout duty. Follow Deedum and see what he gets up to off the clock."

"Sounds riveting."

"You could break into a secure facility with a bunch of criminals if you would prefer."

He put his hands on his ears. "I'm not hearing any of this. Good luck, though. I think you'll need it."

"It would be nice to have some good luck for a change. As of late, I keep getting the bad kind."

CHAPTER TWENTY-TWO

The location Caterpillar gave me to get help with infiltrating Black Jack Security was a place called the Grotto in Eastern Wonderland, above the Thread, but before it got really nice in the north of Wonderland. They wouldn't give me a car, so I found a Zipcar to make my way across the city.

The whole area was built around an enormous arboretum willed to the city by Phineas Thatch III back before the Red Queen's rule. There was a gigantic fountain at its center featuring hundreds of clams, oysters, and other sea creatures dancing ecstatically into the mouth of a massive walrus spitting water at its center.

It was weird, but the whole Thatch family was filled with weirdos, and that was saying something given that all of Wonderland lived in a psychedelic world at one point, but even by Wonderland standards, the remaining family was a weird bunch, not to mention they tripped balls every second of every day. When I was a beat cop, I found the younger grandson, Phineas Thatch VII, passed out in their eponymous fountain. Nearly every NARCO had a story about them.

I wasn't destined for the arboretum, though. No, my route took me around the giant square that housed it and through a series of winding roads that seemed like they were designed by a bunch of high architects. For a city that spent a large portion of its history high as fuck, it was relatively well-maintained, but sometimes, you fell into a loop that showed you how messed up things were for a long time. Streets that dead-ended with no warning and then folded back on themselves, one-way streets that switched directions right in the center, and buildings that felt like they would fall over any second, yet stood for years.

I parked at the edge of a looping street and walked up to a small triangular building in the middle of a cul-de-sac that stood out from the other buildings in that it was literally in the middle of the street, surrounded by asphalt on all sides. It took a special type of person to live in such a maddening place. I wasn't sure I wanted to meet the person behind the door, but I knocked anyway, though it was hard to believe anyone could hear me through the trap music playing so loudly it vibrated the whole structure.

When there was no answer, I knocked again, this time hard enough that even some of the neighbors looked out of their windows. Finally, the music stopped, and feet scuttled to the door. The door opened, and a short, hairy man walked outside—waddled was more like it—and stared at me through large, Coke-bottle glasses.

"You Alice?" he asked sneakily.

"Detective Liddell, yes. And you're Dodo? Like the extinct bird?"

"Exactly like that, because I'm the only one of my kind. Now, come inside before you cause somebody to have a heart attack. We don't like narcs here, and you reek of fuzz."

He pushed me inside the house with greasy hands that looked as if they had just downed a complete pizza without seeing a napkin. The inside of the house was filled with wires running across every surface, running up to the center of the pyramid, with an enormous bank of computer monitors in front of us. It was the kind of place you saw in corny hacker movies, and yet there I was, seeing it in the flesh.

"Don't touch anything," Dodo said, skittering back to his computer chair.

I stepped over a bundle of cables and realized that I didn't see any sort of bed, or kitchen, or bathroom, as there were no doors in the whole place. "It's quaint."

"It sucks, and I know that, but this spot has the absolutely fastest internet in all of Wonderland, so you take the good with the bad, even when there's a lot of bad. The people who designed this place were completely fucked in the head, but then, that's why I like it here. In a world where nothing makes sense, neither does this place."

I kicked a box on the ground and looked down to see a pizza box with two slices of pepperoni remaining. "There's a charm to it, hobo chic or something like that."

"I only work here. I don't live here."

"Of course not. You probably live near the second-fastest signal in Wonderland."

He spun in his chair. "That's right. How did you know?"

I shrugged. "Wild guess."

"I hope you brought a bottle to piss in"—he pointed to the corner of the room where a half dozen bottles filled with yellow liquid sat, and I shivered with disgust—"because we're going to be here a while."

"Gross."

CHAPTER TWENTY-THREE

The only reason Caterpillar would have wanted me to hang out with Dodo was because he was a sadist who wanted to punish me. After two hours of sitting on the disgusting floor filled with old food and piss, the only thing I had to show for my time was a world record for holding my breath from his constant pizza farts.

"Have you found anything yet?" I asked.

"I've found many hundreds of things, but they aren't what you are looking for. Every time I probe the system to find a weakness, it adjusts to me, strengthening places I thought were weak and weakening places that were strong a second before." He turned to me. "However, while it might not seem like anything to you, every single probe teaches me something new. It's only a matter of time before its secrets open to me."

"And do you think that's going to be tonight, or in two weeks, or a year, because I kind of thought we were breaking into a building tonight, so I brought my sneaking boots."

"So pedestrian." He rolled his eyes and started working again. "Everything is in the cloud now, which means all data is hackable. There's no need to go anywhere to do what can be done from the comfort of your own house."

I didn't have the energy or desire to argue with him, which was fortuitous because, at that moment, my phone rang with a call from Arthur. "I'm going outside to take this."

And breathe fresh air.

I pushed open the door and took a deep gasp of the crisp night air before answering the phone and listening to Arthur frantically babble at me. "Are you okay? Oh my god. What happened? Did you call the police? Of course, you are the police, so that brings its own—"

"Arthur!" I shouted. "Breathe."

He did. "I'm sorry. I'm at your place, and I saw your door."

"First things first. What are you doing at my place? Did I call you?"

"No," he replied. "I was just stopping by to see—"

"Stopping by is a thing boyfriends do, not a thing booty calls do. Booty calls wait until their booty is called. It's right there in the name."

"I know, but I thought"—he sighed—"I'm sorry. I guess I'm the asshole for worrying if you are okay."

"No, it's…I'm sorry, okay? Today has been a bad day, and it's not getting any better."

"Is there anything I can do?"

I looked back at the door and sighed. "Trust me. You want no part of this."

"If you're in trouble—"

"I'm not in trouble." I sighed again. There was no better time than now to ruin our relationship by complicating things. "I actually have something I need to ask you, and it's going to sound like it's coming out of left field given what I just said, but I need you not to freak out, okay?"

The concern in his voice was palpable. "Anything."

I took a deep breath. "Can I stay at your place tonight?"

His concern turned to joy in an instant. "Really?"

"Yes, it's just—Dinah offered, but I don't have the energy for her kids right now, and I don't want to be a dick and ignore them. It will be until I can figure out the front door."

"Of course, you can stay with me," he said. "But I don't understand. I thought you didn't stay at men's houses."

"It's not often that my door is kicked in either. You know what, forget it. If you're going to get weird about it, I'll get a hotel or something."

"No, no, no, no, no. I'm sorry. This is just…very exciting, but I can be chill about it."

I laughed. "Are you kidding me? You have forced me into bare-knuckle, drag-out fights because you wanted to move our relationship to another level, and I didn't. I have a hard time believing you won't be weird about this."

"I know you think that, but trust me when I say the only thing I like more than being with you is proving you wrong."

I smiled. "I have to admit, that does sound an awful lot like you."

"Just give me a couple of hours to get my house in order, and then I'll give you a call, and you can come over."

"I really don't care if you're a slob."

"It's not that. I collect *Star Wars* toys and build Legos. I wanna put all that away."

"Oh, you're a nerd. Yeah, you definitely want to hide that stuff from me then. Seriously, Arthur? What kind of girl do you take me for?"

"I don't know. You won't tell me anything about yourself."

"Well, I like *Star Wars*, and though I haven't built Legos in a while, I like puzzles, and they are kind of the same thing."

He stopped for a second. "I really want to say something to you right now, but I won't because I don't want to scare you off, so I'll just say that's fucking awesome. When are you coming over then, because seriously, I do need to clean? I am a filthy slob."

"I'm not sure when I'll be done here, but I'll text you, okay?"

"I look forward to it."

The call hadn't been over for more than ten seconds before Dodo poked his head outside, the stench of farts and old pizza wafting back into my nose. "Are you done talking to your boyfriend because I think I found something?"

"Lead the way," I said before inhaling a big whiff of fresh air and walking back inside after him.

CHAPTER TWENTY-FOUR

"What did you find?" I asked when I entered the fart-infested bungalow.

"It's what I didn't find that matters," he said, waiting for a second to see if I was impressed with his wordplay. When he realized I wasn't, he continued, "I ran a DDOS attack on the server a half dozen times and got thrown back every time. I went to more complex methods, but I circled back around to it and found a vulnerability. Before the system could patch it, I burrowed a worm deep inside their root directory to leave that vulnerability open for us until we could find what we need. It will be discovered eventually when the system rescans its boot drives, but we should have a couple of minutes. What do you need?"

"I didn't understand any of that," I replied. "But you're basically saying we have access to their system, right?"

He sighed. "You NARCOs are all the same. I'm surprised nobody has been able to take down your whole system with how dense you all are."

"We have eggheads of our own. They just aren't me. Now, are we in, or aren't we?"

"Yes, and we should stop wasting time."

"I couldn't agree more," I replied. "I need files on anyone who was on duty around the Looking Glass Lounge two nights ago."

"That shouldn't be too hard. I just need to pull up their duty rosters." He clicked a bunch of buttons as he muttered to himself. "And if it's anything like—yup, here they are. Do you want me to pull them all down or just the ones you need?"

"Whichever will take the least amount of time and leave the smallest footprint."

He tapped again. "These files are all encrypted. I'm going to have to take them all and have you sort it out later. You'll need access to a program that can read .cpw files, but that's on you to figure out. Anything else?"

"Anything you can find about their finances, or"—an idea hit me like a brick—"a client list would be great."

"I'll see what I can do." His eyes darted to the edge of the monitors. "We don't have much time before they purge us and reboot the system."

"Then you should hurry," I whispered to him. "I thought you were the best."

"You should be lucky I got in here at all." He wiped his brow. "Okay, I have them. We have to get out of here now."

"Wait. I thought of one more thing. Can you find any records relating to an incident between Jack Fowler and Councilwoman Lane?"

"You're asking a lot, but—" He took a deep breath. "Found it. There's only one video file. I have it, but they— wait, what is—oh shit!"

The screens around him turned red, and the speakers squealed. He began the type furiously as my eyes ping-ponged between his monitors. "What's happening?"

"No, no, no, no, no," he replied. "They must have it booby-trapped for intruders. When I grabbed that file, it sent a spike that's trying to fry my computer."

"We can't leave without that file!" I shouted.

"We're already out. They locked us out of the system, and now they're trying to access my computer system."

"Did you get it, though?" I asked frantically.

"Yeah," he said. "I got everything, but they might fry my system before we can look at it."

"Don't you have it backed up on an external system, like the cloud or something?"

"Are you kidding?" He was now furiously typing on his keyboard, to the point where I thought the keyboard would break in half. "I don't trust any other servers but the ones I own, and these motherfuckers are trying to wipe them out!"

With that, the entire bank of monitors flashed, and then a smile appeared on the screen with the text *WE SEE YOU.*

"What does that mean?" I asked, confused.

He sighed. "I hope you like your information on file with Black Jack because they just took a picture of us, and I'm sure they're going to the police right now."

"I don't know about that," I said. "Something tells me they have other ways of fixing their problems."

Dodo growled and pulled the computer case out from under his desk. He grabbed a screwdriver from the table and started to unscrew it. "I really loved this place."

"No offense, but I don't know why. It's a shithole."

He spun to me with anger in his eyes. "Yeah, but it was my shithole."

When he was done screwing off the case, he slid out the hard drive and placed it in a metal contraption before handing it to me. "Hold this."

"What am I doing with it?"

"That's everything on this hard drive. If the files are salvageable, then they're on that disk. Open it in a secure location not connected to the internet."

"Isn't there, like, sensitive data on here for your company?"

"Please, I back up my hard drive constantly and wipe it clean every night in case something like this happens. I ran a cloned version of my home laptop to—"

I held up my hand. "I beg of you, no more computer lingo. You can just tell me no, and that's enough."

"Oh, I'm sorry, was this too unpleasant for you? You are a bitch, do you know that?"

"All too well." I let out a sigh. "What are you going to do?"

He stood and went outside. When he returned a second later, it was with a canister of gasoline. "Oh, I'm prepared for this eventuality."

Dodo doused the whole of the room with the gasoline and lit a match. The fire was already halfway up the walls before we were out the door. We crossed the street and watched it burn.

"Pretty smart finding a house in the middle of a cul de sac so the fire won't spread."

"I'm a criminal, not an asshole." He turned to me. "Hey, can you give me a ride? I kind of don't have a license."

I shook my head. "You are a weird dude, Dodo, but sure."

CHAPTER TWENTY-FIVE

I dropped Dodo off at a small coffee shop in the Thread and continued to the department. It was the middle of the night, so I figured I would have until morning before Black Jack Security took action against me. Even if they woke Mr. Deedum out of bed, he would have to at least put on pants and drive to the office to figure out who I was, and that's if they took a good picture of me. Hell, they might have been faking the whole thing to make them look like big, scary security people and not rubes who got hacked.

I decided to park on the street in case I needed to make a fast exit, then headed into the station. I didn't look anyone in the eyes as I rushed to the elevator and took it down to the sub-basement where forensics was located. N'baka rarely slept, and he was a workaholic. He slept sometimes during the morning, but he was always wide awake during the middle of the night.

"Oh good," I said when I saw him at his desk. "I was hoping you would be a degenerate like me."

"Nighttime is the right time for getting shit done," N'baka said with a big smile. "Nobody to bug me, except you, of course."

"I need your help."

"Oof, I can tell. That look on your face—did you murder somebody?"

I held up a hard drive. "No, but I definitely have some records from Black Jack Security that I recovered using less than savory means. Do you have a computer that's not connected to the internet?"

"You're going to get me arrested, aren't you?" He cocked his head to one side. "You know I wouldn't do well in jail, right?"

"I'm not going to get you arrested because I'm not going to tell you what happened, just that I recovered this hard drive. If anybody is going down, it's me."

He thought for a moment, weighing his options before snatching the hard drive from me. "Damn, that is too juicy. You really know how to bait a hook."

He led me to the back of the lab and into a small closet-sized room behind it. Inside was a tiny desk with an ancient monitor that took up half the space, leaving little room for the keyboard and mouse in front of it. N'baka reached into the case under him and pulled out several wires, connecting them to the hard drive before turning on the computer.

"What are we looking for?" he asked, typing onto the keyboard.

"The person I got this from seemed to think the hard drive was compromised, corrupted, or some other type of thing that prevented it from being accessed, but if we opened it on an unconnected computer, we might be able to recover what was inside it."

"And what's inside it again?"

"Records from Black Jack Security revealing who was on assignment the night one of my cases died."

"You really think a multimillion-dollar security company would put a hit out on some lowly criminal?"

"How have you worked here so long, and you're still so naïve? The only people I think would put a hit out on somebody under Caterpillar's protection is a multimillion-dollar corporation who thought they were more powerful than the gods."

"I think you have been drinking conspiracy juice," N'baka said. "I analyzed that card you gave me and didn't find any residue or information that made me think that it was some sort of calling card for an international criminal enterprise."

"Right, the card." I had completely forgotten about it in the fracas of the past few days. "It was a suicide jack, though, right?"

He nodded. "It was, but"—he eyed me for a moment—"you don't play poker, do you?"

I shook my head. "No. I gamble enough with my life to care about a stupid game."

"While this is booting up, let me show you something." He walked out of the room and opened a drawer, pulling out two decks of playing cards. He shuffled through them and threw four cards out. Each of them was a black suicide jack. "These are the cards they're using for the World Series of Poker this year. Most popular cards on the market, in honor of the thirtieth anniversary of the Red Queen's arrest."

I walked forward and pulled up the card. Sure enough, it was the exact same card I remembered from inside William's stomach. I flipped over the card to find a smiling picture of the queen on the back, tiled into the back, smiling at me, like she knew something I didn't.

"Well, fuck."

He patted me on the shoulder. "At least you didn't risk your entire career for nothing."

And that's when I got a text from the captain. *Get to my office. Right now.* Only one thought rushed through my head.

There goes my career, right down the toilet.

CHAPTER TWENTY-SIX

"Do not stop working," I said to N'baka as I walked to the door. "I don't care if the wolves of Hell come to your door. Keep working."

N'baka scratched his head. "No offense, Alice, but I'm not doing that. I like you, but not enough to lose my job. That said, I'll keep working until they physically come and shut me down. I hope that's good enough for you."

I shrugged. "It has to be."

I couldn't honestly expect much from N'baka. We weren't even really more than work friends. I never met his family or went to his house. I asked about his life in passing, but our relationship was transactional, and he just solidified that point for me.

I wasn't in any great rush to get upstairs and find out my fate, so I took the stairs slowly enough that Aman sent me a second text. *I know you are in the building. I'm not fucking around. Get here now.*

I was already fired or at least going to be suspended when I reached the office, and Aman was clearly at maximum pissed off, so making him wait wasn't going to do anything except give me a couple of minutes to collect my thoughts.

Was there a plausible explanation for why I was at a hacker's house as he broke into Black Jack Security's database? Maybe I could say I was there to arrest him, but he got away. No, I was way too relaxed in that picture to be able to say something like that. Although, it did give my attorney plausible deniability in my hearing.

Shit. I needed to text her.

I pulled out my phone and texted my attorney. *Sorry to wake you. Need help now. At 91ˢᵗ precinct.*

She wouldn't be happy with me, but at least she didn't give me a disappointed lecture like my last lawyer. That guy was the worst.

I stopped on the stairwell after climbing two flights and looked up at the light coming from the doorway above me. If it were the light of salvation, it would have been perfectly white, but it was warped by the fluorescent light into a muddled yellow, corrupted by Wonderland, just like everything else.

I took a deep breath, in and out, before placing my foot on the next step. My body fought against me as I worked to push myself up, or maybe it was my unconscious mind fighting my conscious one, knowing what was best for me even when I couldn't conceive it for my own self. It wouldn't be the first time my mind was in conflict with myself in my life. I made a habit of failing my better nature, so I knew that if I forced my way through sheer stubbornness and force of will, my body would succumb to me.

With a sudden jerk, I lunged forward and rushed up two more stairs and then the rest of the way. *Don't think about it. Just do it.*

Perhaps that should have been the slogan of my life, at least recently. If I could have simply taken the time to think about what was best for me, then I would have never chased the March Hare to begin with and never fallen in with Caterpillar at the Looking Glass Lounge. I wouldn't have been in his pocket when he called me to stop a gang war, and I would never have been at that house to force twenty of my fellow officers to die for me.

But I didn't think, did I? Not nearly enough, at least. I pieced things together on the fly and was very good at that, but once the puzzle was solved, I needed immediate action without a moment of forethought because forethought was boring. For as good as I was with solving puzzles, I never liked chess, or Risk, where you had to strategize a dozen moves in advance.

Had I that power, I would likely not be a pariah in the department. I would be able to strategize instead of being a complete idiot.

When the light hit my face, I squinted. How long had I been in that stairwell? It felt like a minute, but when I looked down at my phone, I saw not only three new texts from Aman but that it had been over fifteen minutes. *Had I lost that much time?*

All eyes were on me as I walked across the station to Aman's office, where he waited with his arms crossed. "I was about to send a search team for you."

"Sorry, I got here as fast as I could."

"We both know that's not true. Get inside."

He moved away, but instead of seeing Mr. Deedum, or Jack Fowler, when his large body stopped blocking my vision from what's behind him, instead I saw a young officer I had only met once, and the police chief, waiting in front of me.

That was a new one.

CHAPTER TWENTY-SEVEN

Wait? What is going on?

I never saw the police chief in the department. He worked odd hours, it was true, but so did I. Chief Morales made his bones in the north of Wonderland and, as such, made powerful friends. He never much had a flair for the actual job, but he sure liked the parties that came with power and used his position to get invited to as many as possible. He would never make commissioner because his fellow narcs didn't like him enough, but he respected Commissioner Inman more than the commissioner respected him and thus tried to mimic everything he did, down to the bribes he took.

"Detective Liddell," Chief Morales said with a deep baritone when he stood up to shake my hand firmly. "Not many people have the balls to keep me waiting."

"I'm sorry, sir," I replied, trying not to wince as he ground my hand like a vice. "The captain didn't tell me you were here, or I would have sped myself up."

"I thought you got here as quickly as possible," Captain Aman said. "Isn't that what you told me?"

"I believe in the Scotty approach to work, Captain. Always tell them you are giving it 100%, but really give them 90%, so you have somewhere to go when necessary."

There was a silence in the room for a long moment until Chief Morales let out a thick laugh that blew through the room. "I like you. Makes this a damned shame."

"Makes what a—" I turned to Aman, who pointed down at his desk, where I found my vial of White Rabbit. "Oh."

"Is this yours?" Aman asked, pointing to the officer standing in the corner, silent and sweating bullets like this was his first meeting with the captain. "Officer Jensen says he found it in your apartment."

I spun to him. "And why were you in my apartment, Officer?"

Officer Jensen eyed Aman, who gave him a nod before taking a deep swallow of his fear and opening his mouth. "Ma'am, it was a crime scene. We were looking for clues as to who ransacked your house, ma'am."

I had to be very delicate here. "And where did you find it?"

"Lying on the ground, ma'am, next to a turned-over dresser near the window in your living room."

Damn, that was where I stashed it. In all the commotion, I had forgotten all about the stupid drugs or that officers would be in my house after I left, even though it was standard operating procedure to send rookies to a crime scene to bag and tag everything the senior officers tagged as important to the crime. Somehow, they all missed that little piece of evidence until Eagle Eye Mcgee found it. *That was it. That was the angle.*

"And every other detective just missed it?"

"Y-y-yes, ma'am. I guess so. I don't—"

"How many days on the force do you have, Cadet? Ten?"

"I don't think that's relevant," Aman said. "Please answer me. Is this yours or not?"

Deny. "Of course, it's not. Don't be stupid. I don't use Rabbit."

"It was found in your house," Chief Morales said. "And given your history, let us just say it makes sense. Really ties everything together, I would say."

I cocked my head to the captain. "Is that what you say, too? You think I'm a druggie?"

"I think you've been different since the incident with the boy." Even he couldn't say I shot that poor kid. "It would make sense if you wanted to forget your woes with Rabbit. You wouldn't be the first cop to find comfort in the stuff, and you won't be the last."

"He's right," the chief said. "You have means and opportunity."

"I hate that stuff." Keep denying. "My father died of Rabbit. He was a junkie, and I lost everything to that crap. I would never—"

"Lower your voice!" the captain shouted. "I am not some insolent worm, I am the chief of this whole department, and I will not be talked to like a dog."

I swallowed my anger and took a deep breath. "I'm sorry, sir. You're right. This is all just a hell of an accusation."

"Enough of this," Aman said. "Go to the lab and take a piss test. If you don't have Rabbit in your system, we'll put this all behind us."

"I can't believe—" I bit my lip, trying to sell it. "Whoever did this is setting me up. You have to believe me."

"Methinks she protests too much," Chief Morales replied.

"I protested once, and it's because you are accusing me of being a junkie. I have every right to defend myself from that."

Aman reached into his desk and pulled out a cup. "Take this to the bathroom, and then bring it to the lab. That's an order from your captain."

I took a breath. My whole life flashed before my eyes, but I couldn't stop it from ending. All I could do was hope my bladder was better than everyone else's at processing Rabbit, and maybe I could beat this charge.

CHAPTER TWENTY-EIGHT

They piss-tested you all throughout the academy, and every month I was a uniformed officer, but things got significantly laxer the longer I was in the department and the higher I climbed in seniority. That was mostly due to our union contracts, which were based on the idea that if we hadn't used drugs in the five years it took for us to become plainclothes officers, then the likelihood that we would do so as we aged was significantly less.

It was to the point where I was only piss-tested randomly once every couple of years, and it had never been a problem for me before because I was clean. I mean, I drank a lot and took sleeping pills sometimes, but none of those showed up on piss tests, which was why so many of my compatriots were raging alcoholics, but very few did cocaine, and even fewer smoked weed since it stayed in your system for over a month.

Every once in a while, you heard of a NARCO testing positive for drugs and being suspended for a couple of weeks while they went through rehab, but we all called it the "party vacation." It usually happened to people who had been deep undercover for years, where the rules didn't apply, and who came back with a wicked addiction to something or another.

I wouldn't be getting a slap on the wrist, though. I had already gotten a slap on the wrist too many times. They didn't call the chief in unless there was a big problem, and my firing would certainly be that, not only with the union but also with the public when they heard that the "killer cop" finally got ousted from the department.

I walked into the bathroom and turned on the spigot for the sink. I ran my hands underneath and then through my hair, trying to wake myself up from this awful nightmare. But this was not a dream; it was my real life. I looked over to the stalls. I was alone in the bathroom, and my instinct was to lock the door and climb through the window, but only the guilty fled the scene of a crime, no matter what the movies said. If I stayed on the run for three more days, then I would have plausible deniability, as the Rabbit would have flushed through my system, but disobeying a superior officer was as much a cause for firing as being high on the job.

Except I was never high on the job. I only ever did it in my spare time, and shouldn't I be able to unwind however I like, even if it's destroying my body? Yes, it might have been hypocritical to be a user with a job to track down users, but I had a job to take down criminals and was on the payroll of a criminal, which was just as bad.

And where was Caterpillar in all of this? I pulled out my phone and dialed his cellphone over and over again but kept getting the busy signal until, eventually, a text came through. *I can't help you with this one. If you get through it, come to me.*

Why could he only help me when it was convenient to him? What kind of partnership were we in if we couldn't depend on each other? Then I remembered we weren't in a partnership. He owned me, and if that became inconvenient, he could throw me away. He did it before, but didn't he say I was the only person he could trust? Maybe that wasn't worth the hassle of putting his neck out for me.

Before I could think of anything else, the door opened to the bathroom, and before I could tell them it was closed,

I recognized the face of Rebecca Sanchez, my union lawyer. "There you are! You didn't say anything, did you?"

"Of course not. You taught me better than that."

She kissed me on the cheek. Her lipstick came off on it like it had just been applied, and she rubbed it off with her thumb. "If I knew you listened so good, I would have told you not to do drugs, idiota!"

"I didn't—"

She stuck her finger in my face. "Don't you lie to me, girlie. They found the drugs in your place."

"That had just been ransacked."

She lowered her hand and narrowed her eyes. "Are you telling me, in the eyes of the gods, that you are innocent? Because if you can look me in the eyes and tell me you didn't do drugs, I'll believe you because you would have to be an even bigger idiot to lie to your lawyer."

I thought for a second and then leaned closer. "Okay, yes, I did it."

"You are an idiot," she whispered into my ear. "Give me the cup."

I did what she asked, and she rushed it into the bathroom. Rebecca had a reputation for doing anything for her clients, but I had no idea she would literally pee in a cup for me, especially in the middle of a police station. She was a meticulously dressed woman with perfectly shiny black hair. I didn't even think she peed. I figured she had it all sucked out of her or something classy like that.

When she was done, she held up the cup. "Did you ever do it at work?"

"Absolutely not."

"Do you swear to the gods?"

"Absolutely."

"Because if you ever did it at work…if you ever endangered this department—"

"I didn't. I swear."

"Good." She handed me the cup. "Then take this."

I slid the top on it. "I can't believe you did that for me."

She washed her hands. "I didn't do it for you. I did it because it's a stupid rule, and the only reason they can ask you to pee in a cup is because they found a loophole in our last contract, so I feel like I failed you. Narcs should be able to do whatever they want in their spare time."

"Well, thank you anyway."

She finished drying her hands and turned to me. "Thank me by staying off that crap. It'll rot your brain. Besides that, I really hate being called into the police station in the middle of the night. I need my beauty sleep to keep all of this up."

"I won't call you again. I promise."

"Don't make promises you can't keep, idiota. You're a troublemaker." She smiled at me. "And troublemakers are always my favorite clients. Now, come on. Let's get that pee down to the lab. Then, we'll have a word with your captain."

"Yes, let's. This is so gross."

CHAPTER TWENTY-NINE

I had never more proudly strutted with pee in my hand than how I walked down to the lab for processing. Since it was in the sub-basement with the rest of the "weird" things, I decided to check in on N'baka—after I washed my hands, of course. *Thoroughly.*

Twice.

He seemed surprised to see me when I stepped foot into forensics. They were also a lab, but they didn't handle the actual processing of biological fluids, just analyzing the results of them. "You're still here. I thought for sure you would be fired by the tone of your voice."

"Not yet, but how are you doing with that drive?"

He shrugged. "I haven't checked it in a little while. Let's go see together."

He led me across the lab and into the small coatroom in the back of it. When he sat down, he had several notifications on his screen. "Ah yes. There seem to be three files that have been infected with different tracers and other worms. The system cleaned them, though, and now it seems that the hard drive is safe to use."

"Great, then can you use it?"

He chuckled. "You really don't care if I get fired, do you?"

"Of course, I care. I also care about taking down Black Jack Security, and right now, that's at the top of my mind."

He pressed several buttons and then unplugged the drive from the computer. "I have a wife and three children that mean the world to me, and while you get me amped about the thrill of solving a case when we're together, I have to think of them."

"I thought you only had two kids?"

"We had a third earlier this year." He sighed, handing the hard drive to me. "This is what I'm talking about. I'm sure you have plenty of criminals to give this to, but it needs to be away from me."

"I understand," I replied. "And I really do appreciate your help. I'm a terrible friend."

He nodded. "We are not friends. We are work friends, and I need to do a better job parsing those two things. I do hope you don't get fired, though. I very much enjoy helping you and your cases. They are always more interesting than the others."

I put the hard drive into my coat and walked back upstairs, where I found Rebecca Sanchez talking to Detective Wilde, a wide-boned man with a big bald spot on the back of his head. "And if you have worked here for more than ten years, you get an extra week of vacation. Did your rep really not tell you about this?"

He scratched his head, embarrassed. "Well, maybe they did, but I kind of tune him out."

"I understand. Bill can go on." She smiled, pressing her hand against his bulging back as she saw me. "Ah, Detective Liddell. You have returned. Ready to save your career?"

"I do like the sound of that."

I found it hard to be confident when I was thumbing a hard drive which was at least a thousand times more likely to get me fired than a drug charge. You could get off a drug charge, but a felony computer fraud is a whole different story. That was a federal crime, and I had little hope for myself if that picture ever got out.

"Gentlemen," she said with a smile when she entered a room before seeing the officer in the corner. "Who is he?"

"That's Officer Jensen," Aman replied. "He found your—"

"He's not material to the facts of the case," she replied, her tone hard and stern. "Dismiss him."

"That's not really your call, Rebecca," Chief Morales replied.

"It's Miss Sanchez to you. And he should not have been here in the first place, but if we are going to be discussing confidential information about my client, I need the room cleared of all but the most necessary personnel. Since you barely ever come to this precinct, you are necessary in none but the most technical sense of the word, but I see no reason why you shouldn't stay…unless you have an early tee time in the morning."

Chief Morales growled at her. "Officer Jensen. You are dismissed."

"Thank you, sir," he said, running out of the room at such speed I could barely track him. The relieved smile on his face went from ear to ear.

"Now," Rebecca said, sliding into the chair. "It is my understanding that you are trying to use this drug test to determine my client's eligibility to be fired."

"We never said that," Aman said.

"Of course not, but it's all about the subtext. She has been in trouble before, and this is such a minor offense that—"

"Minor!" Chief Morales said. "She's a junkie!"

"Excuse me," Rebecca said. "She had drugs in her house. There is no evidence she used them. She might have needed them for a case." *Shit. Why didn't I think of that?* "Hell, she might have even tried it to make sure it was pure, and now it's in her system. Seriously, how obtuse can you be?"

Aman chuckled. "You are very good, Reb—Miss Sanchez, and you are legendary for keeping bad narcs on the force, but we both know she is using…but if she isn't, then she will be cleared, and we won't say another thing about it."

Rebecca stood. "When it comes back clean, I hope you offer her an apology."

"I will do that." Aman smiled. "By the way, I heard congratulations are in order. When is the due date?"

I didn't know she was pregnant, and I knew it flustered her, but to her credit, she stayed cool as ice. "I barely told my boss last week. How did you find out?"

"Oh, you know how these things get around," he replied. "You look great. Barely showing at all."

"You only have to eat two-hundred extra calories a day to support a baby, Captain. Most women use it to pig out, which is their right, but I have no interest in that."

"You have very good genes." He waited until we were by the door before he continued. "You know those types of hormones come up on urine tests, right?"

Rebecca's eyes went wide for a second. "Only if you check for them, Captain. Do you suspect Alice to be pregnant?"

He shrugged. "I don't know, but we should check, just to be safe."

"You don't have permission to do that," I said, trying to swallow my frustration. "I forbid it."

"You can't, little lady," Chief Morales said. "Besides, I thought you would be happy. If you're pregnant, then you'll bring a big bundle of joy into this world. Won't that be nice?"

Rebecca turned me around toward the door. "Just go. We'll talk about it outside."

"Goodbye, Detective. I'll let you know the results tomorrow morning. We'll make sure to expedite them for you."

CHAPTER THIRTY

"Shit, shit, shit, shit, shit!" Rebecca screamed when we were safely across the street and out of sight from the police station. "Mierda."

"What were they talking about, Rebecca?" I asked. "It sounded like they knew—"

"Of course, they knew. Shit. I thought I was so careful." She found the confused look on my face. "What, you can't think you were the only client I peed in a cup for, do you?" She must have seen on my face that I really did believe that because she cupped my hands in hers. "Oh, you poor, naïve thing. Didn't you see how quickly and easily I did it? There was no convincing at all, and while I like you, it's not like you're my most important client."

I pulled back. "Then why did you do it?"

"You don't get a reputation of doing everything in your power for your clients without breaking a few stupid rules. How do you think I drive a 7-series BMW? It's not because I'm a shitty defender. It's because I get people off, sometimes literally."

"Gross."

"Oh, please." She brushed her suit. "It's nothing. It's nothing. Or it *was* nothing because they figured it out. How the hell did they figure it out?"

"I don't care how they figured it out. I care about what it means for me."

She turned to me. "Well, you better care about it because I'm the only thing standing between you and the unemployment line, and if you get fired from here for being a junkie, then do you think anywhere in this country will hire you with that kind of thing on your record?"

"I hadn't thought about it. Is it worse than killing a kid?"

"Absolutely. You killed that kid in the line of duty. It was a messed-up thing to do, but you were a good cop in a bad situation. If you're a junkie, you're a liability, and suddenly people start asking if the two things are connected."

"But they're not!"

"And nobody cares about that." She cleared her throat. "The best thing you can do is go home and wait this out. How long until the shit is out of your system?"

"A couple of days," I replied.

"Then, for the gods' sake, don't go back to work or get anywhere near a crime scene until you are clean. Turn off your phone, don't answer your messages, and call out sick to work. No matter what, do not talk to Aman until you are clean. Do you know where to get home testing kits for drugs?"

I nodded. "Yeah, I've given them to some people over the years."

"Good." She grabbed my shoulder. "We can still get through this, but you have to trust me."

"I do," I replied with a smile. "You are one of the few people who have always been on my side."

"That's because I'm the best, and your union pays me good money. Now, get some sleep, okay?"

I nodded, and she walked away. I turned back to the station to get my car but thought better of it. It was possible Aman was waiting for me, or he could track my car when I took it out of the precinct. I was better off taking the subway for a couple of days. Maybe I should leave my phone at home. Even if I got fired for it, that would be better than being fired for drugs.

Or maybe I should quit. If I quit, then they couldn't drug test me…unless they arrested me, of course, which was possible since they all hated me, and there was a picture floating around of me committing felonies.

This day kept getting better and better, and just when I thought it had come to another head, I got a phone call from an unknown number. I let it ring through, but then the phone vibrated with a text. *Answer your phone. – Deedum.*

Shit. When the phone rang again, I had no choice but to pick it up. "Is this your doing then? Are you calling to gloat?"

"I'm not answering questions. I don't know what you took. Just bring it to me."

"I'm not your puppet."

"I know, but I know who is pulling your strings, and if you want to remain a free girl, you'll do as I say. Meet me in the lobby of the office. Ten minutes."

"I don't have a car."

"Then make it thirty. And whatever you do, bring every copy you have, or I'll make your life very unpleasant."

"I have a newsflash for you; it's already unpleasant and getting more unpleasant by the second."

"Good, that makes my heart sing a little bit, knowing your life sucks, but trust me, I can make it much, much worse."

The phone cut off, and I screamed into the ether. I was already a puppet for one strong man, and now, it seemed like I was being set up to be a puppet for a second one, and I didn't like it. No, I didn't like any of this, and that was the understatement of the year, maybe the decade, and possibly the century.

CHAPTER THIRTY-ONE

As I walked to the subway line to meet with Mr. Deedum, I clocked a shadow following me in the distance. It didn't exactly try to keep itself hidden, but it kept to the darkness when possible. As my legs scurried forward, the shadow moved faster as well, until I was close to breaking out in a sprint, and the shadow was on top of me.

"Alice," a familiar voice said from the shadows.

I turned to see Dormouse's massive frame shining in the street light.

"We need to talk," he said.

"I don't have time for this. I'm late for a meeting."

"Going to meet your dealer?" he asked.

"I'm not a junkie, asshole. And no, I'm not going to meet my dealer. I don't even have a dealer."

"Don't lie to me, Alice. It would explain a whole hell of a lot about your volatility the last few months."

"Oh, would it? I'm sorry me dealing with killing a kid was too fucking volatile for you."

"That's not what I meant."

I stepped forward. "You abandoned me when I needed you most, so you have no right to lecture me about my life choices."

"I didn't abandon you. I stayed your partner beca—"

"Out of pity." I felt hot tears streaming down my face. The last thing I wanted to do was cry in front of him, but I didn't have a choice. My body couldn't fight the pain coursing through it anymore. "You told me you thought I should quit. You said I made your life—" I bit my lip hard enough that it drew blood, then winced at it. "Don't pretend to be my friend now."

Dormouse reached into his pocket and pulled out a handkerchief. "I am your friend. I'm just a terrible one, and that has everything to do with me and nothing to do with you." He stopped. "You killing that kid put a lot of things into perspective for me. It wasn't easy for me, you know."

"Poor you," I growled at him as I dabbed the handkerchief on my bleeding lip.

"I was a kid too, once, Alice, and I have kids that look an awful lot like the kid you killed. Or didn't you think about that?"

I hadn't, and he was right. Dormouse grew up not far from the sight of the shooting, and his kids grew up in the Thread for a couple of years until they could afford a place outside the city with better schools and less violence.

"I…I didn't."

"Well, maybe you were a bad friend, too. You never once checked in to see how I was doing, but you had no problem making yourself the center of the world, and yet you aren't the center of the world, Alice. This whole story isn't about you. It's about all of us, and we're all doing more than playing a part. When I leave here, I have to go home to my wife and children. I have to look them in the eyes and know that my partner killed somebody the same age, with the same color eyes and the same color skin."

"Are you calling me a racist?"

"No, I'm not. I'm calling you obtuse because you didn't think about any of this, and yes, I'm saying that I lashed out at you because I can't close my eyes without seeing you killing my kid instead of that poor boy, killing me instead of that poor boy. You know I worked late when I was his age, stocking groceries just like him, to help put food on the table."

Now, we were both crying, and I brought him close to me. "I'm sorry, Dormouse. I'm so sorry. I didn't think about it. I just—I thought—I had my head up my own ass."

"Yeah, you're good at that." He pushed back from me. "And if you were on drugs that whole time, it goes a long way to explaining what the fuck happened that night and what the hell has been going on since you came back."

I sighed. "I wish I could help you, Dormouse, but I didn't start using until after the incident, and even then, it was only to help take the edge off and get to sleep. I never did it on the job."

"But you did do it, right?"

I bit my lip. "Gods help me, I did it, okay? I know it was a shit thing to do, but fuck man, I have had a pretty shit couple of months, and it just keeps getting worse."

Dormouse stepped back. "If you're not going to your dealer, then where are you going?"

"I can't tell you. If I do, it'll implicate you, and I can't have that."

"Gods damn it, Alice. I'm already implicated. How do you think it looks that I didn't know my own partner was using drugs? How hard do you think they'll come down on me this time? I barely survived the last shitstorm you threw at me. They'll bust me down to beat cop next time if they don't kick me off the force completely. We're in this together, whether I know what's going on or not. I want to know what's going on, so I can seal my own fate."

"I'm going to Black Jack Security to see Mr. Deedum." I pulled the hard drive out of my coat. "To give him this."

"I don't want to know what's in there, do I?"

I shook my head. "Absolutely not."

He gritted his teeth. "All right then. Let's go."

"No," I replied. "I have to go alone."

He smiled deviously. "You act like you have a choice in the matter. Either you come with me, or I'll take that from you and give it to the captain. Something tells me you don't want that."

I didn't, but I didn't want to get Dormouse in trouble either. Rock, meet hard place. "Fine, it's your life, but don't say I didn't warn you."

"Good," he replied. "I'll go get the car."

"I'm fine with the subway."

He turned from me. "I'm not. If you leave before I get back, I'll send half the department after you, got it?"

I nodded. "I'll be here when you get back."

"You better."

CHAPTER THIRTY-TWO

The wind whipped through my coat and chilled my bones as I waited for Dormouse. What were the odds that he would bring the police to me anyway? He had been a true friend once, but if things were as dire as he said they were, wouldn't it be more logical to feed me to the wolves than help me commit a crime? Or was he waiting for a crime he could arrest me for and be seen as a hero—the cop that stood against his villainous partner?

That sounded like him. He was a boy scout that way, but he was also pragmatic. If he turned on one crooked cop, every other crooked cop would turn on him. He always had a way of playing both sides against the middle and finding ways to make all the corrupt NARCOs like him, even if he wasn't one himself. I doubted he wanted to risk ruining that reputation.

Even if I was wildly disliked, the stink of corruption wafted off me, and now that Dormouse knew I was working for Caterpillar, he wouldn't risk his family to take me down knowing I was protected, would he?

The wind rankled my bones and sent every part of my body to stand on edge. I felt like a prey animal, trying to avoid the prying eyes of hawks and other predators hungry to take me down. Every minute I spent near the NARCO station allowed for the possibility of somebody finding me and forcing me back inside.

I wasn't a criminal yet, but the minute they knew Rebecca substituted her pee for mine, they would force me to do another test in front of them, and then they would know the truth. It was stupid for me to wait for him. Even if he hated me for it, that was a far cry better than the possibility of being found out.

Besides, even if he did show up and whisk me away, it was to do crimes. I was about to admit to Mr. Deedum that I hacked into his system, and bringing Dormouse implicated him in the crimes, too. Even if he chose to remain silent, that would make him an accessory after the fact. After all I had done to him, I couldn't take that chance.

I'm sorry, Dormouse, but this is for your own good.

I turned toward the subway but hadn't taken three steps before the distinct sound of Dormouse's engine filled the air, and bright headlights shined on me. "Going somewhere?"

"No," I lied. "I'm just cold. You left me in the cold, Dormouse."

"Well, it's warm in here. Get in."

It wasn't so much an invitation as a command, and I dutifully followed it, getting into the car I rode in hundreds of times before. But this time, I felt more like the criminal than the NARCO agent, and Dormouse felt like my warden above anything else.

"So, tell me how you got involved in drugs in the first place."

"Jesus, Dormouse. Buy a lady dinner first."

"I'm sorry, but if I'm going to help you, then I need to know the truth."

"I don't want your help. I'm not some damsel that needs saving."

"You are a woman, thus damsel, and you fucked up, thus you need saving."

"I can slay my own dragons."

"You can chase your own dragons."

I slapped him on the arm. "Fuck all, Dormouse. I'm not on heroin. I did a little Rabbit to take the edge off."

"Yes, that's how it starts, now spill."

I opened my mouth to sigh, but as I did, it all started to fall out of my mouth. "Getting reassigned was the straw that broke the camel's back, Dormouse. This job is all I had ever known, and I realized I'm terrible at it."

"You're not a terrible cop," he replied. "You're a great cop."

"In the span of three months, I was responsible for the deaths of over thirty people."

"And I was responsible for one less than you, so does that make me a bad cop?"

"Of course not," I replied.

"I'm just trying to figure it out because it seems to track that if you're a bad cop, so am I."

"Fuck, man. You want me to tell this story or not?"

"Sorry," he replied. "But I'm not a bad cop."

"Fine. I concede that."

"And neither are you."

"Whatever. Listen, what I'm saying is that was the topping on a shit sandwich, and it made me spiral, so I got some Rabbit from a dealer I know, and it sat there for days and days until one day, I snapped, and I took it. Just a bit before bed, and it opened my eyes to all sorts of shit."

"Yeah, I have heard that before," he scoffed.

"That's because it's true. You've never done Rabbit, Dormouse, but fuck, man. It was a trip, a literal trip to another world where nothing mattered, and I wasn't a world-class screw-up, and I hadn't just killed a bunch of people. It was kind of fucking great, but I was careful. I knew the risks, so I did it a little bit at a time, disappearing into Wonderland for thirty minutes or less, but gods damn it, man. It was fucking great."

"You certainly sound like a junkie."

My head snapped to him. "I'm not a junkie. I'm just fucking sick of this."

"Sick of what?" he asked as if he didn't know.

"All of this bullshit. Every day, waking up and getting hammered by life every second of every minute. It fucking sucks, and when I'm in Wonderland, nothing else matters. I can just live, free and clean."

"But you're not clean. You're on drugs."

"You know what I mean." I turned away from him. "You know, people lived in Wonderland for a long time and didn't have anything bad happen to them. It wasn't so bad until we started to regulate it."

"That's bullshit, and you know it. Living in a fantasy world is worse than living in reality, even if they have cute animals and talking flowers and shit."

I dropped my head. "I'm not sure I agree with you. Maybe the Red Queen was right. Maybe it was better back then when we didn't have to put up with any of this bullshit."

"That's crazy. You're talking like an insane person."

"Not if you were there, Dormouse. If you saw what I saw, you would think it's the only way to live after all the shit I've seen."

"Don't ever let anyone else hear the shit you just said. They will string you up for supporting the Red Queen."

"I don't support her. I just don't think she was wrong."

"In Wonderland, that's the same thing."

CHAPTER THIRTY-THREE

We stayed quiet the rest of the way to Black Jack Security. The lights were off in most of the other buildings, even the one that held their offices, except for some security lights in the lobby and bright lights coming from high in the tower.

I expected the door to be locked, but instead, a burly security guard was waiting at the door, trying her best not to fall asleep. "Detective Liddell?"

I nodded. "That's me."

"Who's the other one?"

"My partner, Dormouse."

"He can't come."

I looked over at Dormouse, who was even beefier than the guard and mean-mugging like a champ. "You can try to stop him, but I've been trying for half an hour, and it hasn't worked."

The guard thought for a minute and then must have realized she doesn't get paid enough to deal with this shit because she let us through and sent us to the elevator. It was made of glass, but there was little to look at in the dim of night, especially in the financial district, which became a ghost town after the markets closed. Some poor saps lived around in the few apartment complexes they built while trying to turn it into a hotspot, but it didn't bring in enough people to warrant bars and restaurants staying open late, so they had to hoof it to other areas if they wanted nightly entertainment.

"You ready for this?" Dormouse asked as we neared the floor.

"I don't even know what to prepare for, so absolutely not. This is my first covert meeting in the dead of night."

"Lies," he replied.

"Yeah, well, it's my first one with somebody that isn't a criminal."

Dormouse chuckled. "Oh, Mr. Deedum is a criminal."

"Yeah, but not the kind that goes to jail."

"He might yet," Dormouse replied. "Have faith."

"Fuck faith. I work in Wonderland. The rich are never punished for their bullshit."

The door to the elevator opened, and Deedum stood in the middle of the hallway, waiting for us. It would have been quite intimidating if I didn't figure he was waiting by the phone in the office for the security guard to tell him we were coming like an eager puppy. I could almost see the tail wagging behind him as he burst with the excitement he tried to contain.

"You're late," he said. "And you brought company."

"It was unavoidable," I replied. "You know how it is when you're framed as a druggie."

He smiled. "That's not fair. You are a junkie. I just made sure your people knew it at the opportune time."

"So, you ransacked my place?"

He shrugged. "It's a bit archaic but effective. I'll bet you haven't felt comfortable since."

"Joke's on you. I haven't felt comfortable in my place for months."

"That's a shame." He waved his hand in the opposite direction of his office. "Please, come in."

There was a lot of fanfare in Timothy Deedum. He could have simply had it out for us in the lobby, but instead, he decided to drag us up to his elaborate offices and weave us through them until we ended up in the conference room.

"I'm very proud of this place. When Jack started this place, we were in a little office behind a deli. It smelled great, but the noise was awful." He looked out the window and stretched his arms. "We went from that to all this, and do you know how we did it?"

"Intimidation and tax evasion?" I asked.

Dormouse chuckled, but Deedum did not. "I can hear the contempt in your voice, Alice, but it's not my fault Wonderland is how it is. It's not my fault the rich control everything, and they pay me to make sure their problems go away."

I pinched the bridge of my nose. "First off, yes, it is. It's your fault because you perpetrate the bullshit all around."

"If not me, then somebody else."

"Maybe, but it doesn't have to be you. No, you decided to infiltrate this system and use it for your own gain."

He turned to me. "So some other shlub could get rich and not me?"

"We all make choices, Timothy, but more importantly, not that you are rich and powerful, you do nothing to help the people of this city."

"We donate millions to charity."

"And how many of those charities are run by your clients?" There was no answer. "Yeah, exactly. Have you ever given a dollar to a bum on the street or thought about how you could help those that couldn't help you back?"

"This is stupid," he replied. "I thought you would be reasonable, but I can see there is no getting through to you, so I will be frank. Give me the files you stole, or this picture is leaked."

He pulled a file out of his jacket and slid it across the table. I didn't have to open it to know what it was, but I did anyway, just to confirm he had a picture of me at the computer with Dodo. "It's a good picture. I wish I smiled, though."

"I don't have to tell you what that is, but rest assured, we have meticulous records that traced a hacker back to their system, and this was the imagery it obtained. We have prosecuted others for much less."

"Is he telling the truth, Alice?" Dormouse asked. "Because if so, you really are a reckless idiot."

"That might be the case," I replied. "But I'm sure there is something on this hard drive which would implicate him or his clients."

"We don't know what's on that hard drive, Alice," Deedum said. "That's the point."

I chuckled. "So, you expect me to believe you know exactly who stole from you but have no idea what I took? I think that's bullshit."

He leaned forward. "And I assume you have a Ph.D. in computer science to back up that bravado."

"No, just a world-class bullshit detector." I slid the folder back over to him. "How do I know you'll destroy the photo if I give you the drive?"

"You don't," he replied. "How do I know that's the only copy of the files you took?"

"You don't. So, I suppose we're at a stalemate?"

"I think not," he said, turning to Dormouse. "Did you get what I asked?"

Dormouse looked at me and then back at Deedum. "Yes, sir."

"What?" I asked, indignant. "What is he talking about?"

"Don't you know?" Mr. Deedum said. "I own everyone."

"You," I replied. "You're the White Queen."

CHAPTER THIRTY-FOUR

Mr. Deedum looked at me dead serious for a moment and then laughed heartily. When he was done, he wiped a tear from his eye. "That was the best joke I've heard all day."

"Don't try to deny it. You said you own everyone."

He shrugged. "Maybe it was a slight exaggeration, but I can say for certain that I am not the White Queen, though I have no love for the Caterpillar you have pegged your allegiance to."

"I don't have any allegiance to him other than the fact that he helped me out of a jam, and I owe him because of it."

"I was not expecting to hear that." He smiled. "Good, that's good to hear, but first. May I please have the recording?"

Dormouse looked at me sheepishly for a moment before walking over to Deedum. He ripped open his shirt and pulled a wire out of it and a recorder he kept in his breast pocket. "Here you go."

Deedum smiled and rewound the tape, clicking play when he was satisfied.

"But you're not clean. You're on drugs."

"You know what I mean. You know, people lived in Wonderland for a long time and didn't have anything bad happen to them. It wasn't so bad until we started to regulate it."

"That's bullshit, and you know it. Living in a fantasy world is worse than living in reality, even if they have cute animals and talking flowers and shit."

"I'm not sure I agree with you. Maybe the Red Queen was right. Maybe it was better back then when we didn't have to put up with any of this bullshit."

"Oh, this is even better than I expected," he said, clicking stop on the tape. "I wanted you to admit you used drugs, but treason is better than I ever could have imagined."

"I wasn't serious," I said. "I was just saying—this is bullshit."

"I told you it was bad," Dormouse said. "Why did you have to defend the queen? If you had just admitted to using drugs, then you would have been fired, but now, you might end up in front of a firing squad."

I was so angry I could have decked Dormouse in the mouth, but I needed to see how this would play out. Who knew what crazy kinds of surveillance Deedum set up and if I was going to get out of this in one piece?

"What do you want, Deedum?" I growled at him. "Let's get this over with."

"Now we get down to the brass tacks of it," he said. "What I want is for you to take down Caterpillar and expose him for the worm he is."

I laughed. "You're kidding, right? You might say you own everyone, but he actually owns everyone, including my boss and my boss's boss, all the way up to the commissioner."

He stopped for a moment, and his eyes narrowed. "I need to show you something."

"This should be good."

He walked over to a keyboard in the corner of the room, and when he typed onto it, the screen on the opposite wall sprung to life. After several clicks of his keyboard, a video popped up and started to play.

On it, I saw William walking down an alley. He went out of the frame and then stumbled backward into it again. He fought against an enormous man. He gave a good fight, but it was no use. The man was enormous and knocked him to the ground. They fought, and the tiger bloodied poor William up, mashing in his face before pulling out a piano wire and choking him out. Before the boy died, the video froze.

"This was deleted from our server during your incursion. Luckily, I had an offline backup. Do you recognize this man?"

He zoomed into the face of the man and pulled it into focus. I saw on the screen the face of a tiger, the exact same one that worked for Caterpillar.

"That can't be—"

Mr. Deedum walked across the room. "Caterpillar is not a good person. He sent you on a wild goose chase to frame me for a murder he committed."

"Why would he do that?"

"Isn't it obvious? He's afraid of me. He knows Jack and I are the most powerful people besides him still loyal to the Red Queen, and I know where all his bodies are buried. He wants to start a war between us, but he needs you to give him cover so that the elite of Wonderland don't turn against him." He walked over to me. "I hoped the video I showed would sway you to help me, but I am keeping the other two pieces of evidence as collateral. Dispose of Caterpillar, and I will destroy these pieces. Deny me, and they will end up on the six o'clock news. You'll not only be a pariah. You'll be the most wanted woman in Wonderland."

I gritted my teeth together. I had no great love for Caterpillar, but I hated being manipulated. Mr. Deedum would pay for this, but first, I needed to take out the trash.

"Fine," I replied. "I'll do it."

"Wonderful. I'm so happy you can be reasonable." He turned to Dormouse. "You told me she would be, and I'm so happy to see you didn't lead me astray."

CHAPTER THIRTY-FIVE

"You don't have to walk me out," I said to Dormouse as he followed me to the elevator. "Haven't you already done enough?"

"Mr. Deedum wants to make sure you don't mess with anything on your way out."

I pressed the button for the elevator, and it opened immediately. I stormed inside, and Dormouse followed me. "So, you're his errand boy now? How long has this been going on?"

He dropped his eyes. "After the explosion, there was a lot of heat on me. I didn't know where to turn, and I needed some backup. Mr. Deedum reached out to me and offered me some work on the side, and it spiraled from there."

"Until you were deep into his pocket?" I asked, feeling a familiar story.

"Exactly."

"Well," I replied, biting the place on my lip that had stopped bleeding, "I fucking hate you, but at least I understand that. I've been there before. I'm sorry you had to go there because of me."

"It would have happened eventually. They don't pay us enough on purpose, I think, so we have no choice but to get into the pockets of somebody." He shook his head. "The deeper I got, the more money there was until I was too deep to dig my way out. Now, he has too much on me for me to stop."

"Sounds like a great guy." The door dinged, and I stepped out into the lobby. "I didn't rip your throat out because of our history, but if I ever see you again…" Tears welled in my eyes as I thought about my oldest friend stabbing me in the back. "Don't let me see you again."

"Don't be like that. Let me drive you home. Maybe we can figure this out."

"I don't want to do anything with you, traitor." I stormed off toward the subway station. "I would wish you dead, but I don't want to do that to Charlotte or the kids."

I made sure he was out of sight before I fell to my knees and broke down. The absolute last thing I expected in this world was for Dormouse to be on the take. He had always been my shining light. But then again, that was a dark time for me, and I could only imagine what it would have been like with a wife and children you had to look out for.

As I cried my eyes out, I wondered how many NARCOs ended up in the same position, down on their luck, needing a friend, and that's when a hand comes down like manna from Heaven, except it wasn't an angel, it was a demon with an expensive suit and smile that made you think everything might be okay.

But nothing was okay. If things were okay, you wouldn't be wallowing in a sewer in the middle of the night, now beholden to two powerful men, each of which had a deep hatred for the other.

I knew I was a cog in a machine when I was a NARCO, but I never felt like a pawn. I never felt like I was being moved on a chessboard by somebody else, trying to get in the right position to win some meta-game, until I could die at the right moment. Well, I would not be sacrificing myself this night or any night. Not for Caterpillar, Mr. Deedum, or any other person drunk on power in this world.

It was time to fight back and create a way to save myself in the process. There was only one other player in this game who had a problem with Black Jack Security and wanted White Rabbit off the street enough to come down hard on Caterpillar and who was powerful enough to clash with them.

Of course, she could also take me down hard if I revealed myself to her, but that was a chance I had to take. I didn't know if Councilwoman Lane was still on my side, but at one point, she said she was rooting for me, so I hoped so.

Otherwise, this would be a short plan that ended with me behind bars for the rest of my life, or worse.

CHAPTER THIRTY-SIX

Showing up at the head of the city council when you were wanted by the NARCOs was a good idea, right? Rebecca told me to stay low, but I needed to work fast before too many things congealed around me, and I was stuck in this situation for much longer. It was an insane gamble, and it meant getting past the guards that stood between the gates and the brownstone where she lived.

It wasn't always so hard to meet with her, but after two failed assassination attempts in the past four years, security was ratcheted up to prevent any idiot from walking past her house, and right now, I was some idiot. It would have been way easier to wait for her to get back to the office and catch her in the parking lot, but I didn't have that kind of time. By tomorrow morning, there would be a concerted effort to find me, so it was either act now or never.

Security started two blocks away from her apartment, where two NARCO units set up cars to block anyone from passing by. The thing that most people didn't know was they were only staffed for two hours in the morning and night every day, always during rush hour, but even their cars being present was enough of a deterrent for most people.

The cars prevented 95% of people from walking past them and getting a closer look at the residence, which made sussing out any possible intruders easier since there was no crowd protecting their route.

Video cameras set up at every corner did most of the other work of stopping people from getting within a block of the residence, which meant you had to walk with authority straight ahead toward the guard tower if you hoped not to be stopped, and even then you would surely be asked what you were doing when you reached the gate.

"Halt!" a booming voice shouted from a guard tower in front of the residence. "State your business."

I held up my badge, hoping it was enough. I was only slightly better at deception than I was at sneaking. My strength lay in the truth, not lies. I could suss out the truth and beat it out of anyone who failed to render it, but the last several months in service to criminals honed my tongue into an impure form of silver and cleaved it down the middle so that it was nearly as forked as a politician's.

"I'm with the NARCO division. I need to talk to Councilwoman Lane right now."

The guard shook her head. "I'm sorry, but she's not accepting visitors."

"This isn't a visit. It's an urgent matter. There are forces conspiring against her that she needs to know about."

The guard's eyes narrowed. "If that's true, then bring your concern to the commissioner, and she can bring it to the councilwoman through the appropriate channels."

"Are you an idiot? The commissioner is deep in the pockets of the people who conspire against her."

The guard rolled her eyes. "All right, crazy person. I'm going to need you to turn around and go away before I arrest you."

"I'm a fucking cop, idiot!" I growled at her. "I'm the one who does the arresting."

I had enough of her. If you walked with enough authority, most people would let you pass, so I decided to press my luck. I stomped forward past the tower and slid under the bar that prevented my entrance, but before I could stand, I felt a hand on my shoulder pulling me back.

The last thing I wanted to do was hit a cop, but desperate times. Before I rose up, I balled my fist and smashed it into the guard's jaw when I stood, clocking her two additional times, one on each cheek, and then a roundhouse kick to the face, knocking her backward to the ground.

By the time I was done, the lights flicked on all over the street, and sirens screamed. I couldn't fail, so I had to take my chances. I pulled off my coat and slid under the bar again, rolling to my feet as two guards pulled guns on me. I rushed forward and threw one of the guards into the other, knocking them back, and then ran over them toward the front door of the house.

Before I could climb the stairs, three more guards rushed out of it, screaming at me to stop. I wouldn't kill a cop, yet I had no other choice but to pull my gun and fire. My hand shook as I went for my gun. It had been a long time since I fired a weapon—since that night with Vincent.

My hand shook as I raised the gun. I went for the trigger, but it was so heavy in my hand that I couldn't pull it. "I don't want to hurt you, but I will."

It was a lie, a bald-faced lie, but I didn't have anything else except the power of my words since the bullets failed to fire from my chamber without my will to pull the trigger.

"Put your gods damned gun down, or I will blow your fucking head off!" one of the men shouted back at me.

From inside, a scream rang out. "What the hell is going on out there?" The curtain flipped open, and for a moment, I saw a blur of a woman look out at me. "Gods damn it. Lower your gun, Harold."

"But ma'am—"

"Now, Harold!" Councilwoman Lane stepped out of the house with a pink silk robe and messy hair. "After all, she doesn't want to kill me, do you Detective Liddell?"

Harold and his men dropped their guns, and I did the same. "No, ma'am. I just need to talk with you."

Councilwoman Lane folded her arms. "Then you should schedule office hours."

I narrowed my eyes. "With all due respect, I asked you to call me days ago, and I haven't heard back, so—"

"I'm busy!" she screamed. "It's on my to-do list."

I stomped forward. "Well, no offense, ma'am, but this is too important to wait for your to-do list."

"Yes, I can see that. And why would you offend me now, after knocking out one guard and wounding two others? Yes, let us stand on ceremony now," she growled. "Well, come in. I'll put on tea, and you can tell me what is so important you would risk your life and those of my men."

"Thank you, ma'am."

"Think nothing of it." She turned to the door. "And Harold, call an ambulance for Clarice and the other men Alice fell. See that she is attended to, and should she have any more than a black eye, make sure Detective Liddell is arrested forthwith."

"And until then?" Harold asked.

"Keep your lips sealed." With that, she walked inside, and I followed her.

"I didn't break any bones, ma'am," I replied. "I am very good."

"Really? Well, let us hope you are a better fighter than a shot because I heard you couldn't hit the broad side of a barn. Good bluff, though."

"Well, desperate times, ma'am."

CHAPTER THIRTY-SEVEN

True to her word, Councilwoman Lane went about preparing tea, never asking whether I even liked tea, which I didn't, or how I liked it prepared, as coffee. She was quite methodical about it, humming to herself as she boiled the kettle and scooped the tea into two floral cups. After pouring the tea, she went into her cupboard and pulled out two plates, along with bread, mayo, cream cheese, and cucumbers from the fridge.

I stayed silent as she mixed the cream cheese and mayo and then spread it on the bread before slicing the cucumbers and placing them on the bread. When the timer went off on the stove, she finished cutting the crusts off the bread and placed them on the table, then put a cup in front of me before taking a seat at the table opposite me.

She took a sip, then noticed I hadn't touched mine. "You should try it. It's not poisoned or anything. I just thought you might be knackered after such a violent outburst." She pushed the plate over to me. "It's my mother's recipe."

I took one of the cubes she cut and took a bite since I didn't want to insult her and was surprised it wasn't the worst thing I had ever tasted. "Thank you."

She leaned back in her chair. "Now, why don't you tell me what you are doing here and why I shouldn't call the commissioner on you right now, Detective Liddell."

"If you call the commissioner, you'll never find the White Queen."

She chuckled. "That is a bold statement. Why do you think I care about this 'White Queen'?"

"You don't have to play coy with me. I know you must have been briefed on her, and I think I have found him hiding in plain sight."

She smirked. "Oh, have you? Do tell."

"I think the person you're looking for, we're all looking for really, is Mr. Deedum, or, more broadly, Black Jack Security. I think they are trying to take over the drug trade from Cat—other sources to expand their power."

"I know Jack quite well, and he doesn't seem like the type."

"Really? He's done dirty work for hundreds of people in Wonderland. You really don't think he would do something like try to control the White Rabbit trade here after he worked so closely with the Red Queen for all those years?"

She sighed. "When you put it like that, I can't say I would be surprised if he were the culprit behind this, but it seems so dastardly, not to mention ingenious, and he's never been the type to hatch a master plot. Be privy to one, yes, but not the mastermind behind it."

I took a sip of tea. She was right. It was quite good. Not as good as coffee, but good enough. "One thing I've learned about the rich is, if they see a way to make more money, they will take it."

"I take exception to that, Miss Liddell. I am rich. Do you think that of me?"

I thought for a moment. "I'm not sure what to make of you, Councilwoman, but once you said you were on my side, and I hope that is still true."

"Well, it was true before you disturbed my sleep and beat up my guards, but now I'm not so sure what to think of you."

I leaned forward. "Know I am a damn good cop. Good enough to know you have a grudge against Jack Fowler."

She put down her tea and stroked her chin. "Is that so?"

"Yes, I know that before you took power, you had a lawsuit against him, and he filed a countersuit"—all of that was just pulled out of my ass, but when I saw the look of shock on Councilwoman Lane's face, I knew I was on to something—"and I know it was settled out of court, but I don't know what it was about, so I was hoping you could tell me. That was the purpose of my first call."

She picked up her tea and took a long sip. "Maybe you are a good detective, just with a penchant for getting involved in bad situations."

"I assure you I am, which is why I know I'm onto something with Black Jack Security."

"What I tell you is never to pass your lips again, for any reason. Am I understood?" When I nodded, she continued. "It's very sticky business, but before I staged my coup of the Lories, Jack came to me with pictures." She sighed. This was hard for her, I could tell. "Pictures of me cheating on my ex-husband. He threatened to go public with it if I didn't withdraw my candidacy."

"So, he was working for the Lories?"

"It would seem that way, yes. He never admitted it, though."

"But didn't they oust the Red Queen from power?"

She chuckled. "Oh, my dear. For all your posturing, you must not know very much about power. Those in power will do anything to keep it, and when power is passed, those who received it are just as interested in keeping their heads as those they deposed. That is what

Jack knows better than anyone and used it to his advantage more than once."

"But you didn't stop your candidacy? Why?"

She chuckled. "Mutually assured destruction, of course. I promised that if he outed me, I would have him arrested for treason. I have documented proof of him contacting the Red Queen after her trial, and we all know what happens to traitors in Wonderland."

"Off with their heads."

She nodded. "The Lories promised amnesty for anyone who gave witness against the Red Queen, but they had to swear never to contact her again and pledge loyalty to the city, so if it came out that he had contact with the Red Queen after his immunity plea…"

"He would go down." She nodded. "What happened?"

"Oh, as always happens, threats became lawsuits became a settlement, and we agreed that we would keep our silver bullets out of the media."

"Mutually assured destruction," I whispered.

"Exactly," she said. "Now, I must know everything you know. Spare no detail. I have a full kettle, and I love a good story."

I didn't want to tell her everything, but I had no choice. I needed her cooperation to protect me from both Black Jack and Caterpillar. She was the only one who had enough juice to keep me safe, so I told her everything, from the moment I killed that poor boy, Vincent, until I came to ask for her aid.

When I was done, she nodded. "I see why you were so desperate to find me."

"Exactly."

Her brows furrowed. "But your story concerns me. If you pulled information off that server related to my dalliances, it means it could get out."

I shook my head. "No way. I told you. I gave the only copy back to Mr. Deedum."

Her eyes narrowed. "You might believe that, but I am not convinced. This computer programmer that helped you could have betrayed you." She finished her tea and placed it down. "If you want my help, then you must bring this Dodo to me, and quickly. Every minute we waste is one that my tawdry information can get out."

"I have no idea how to track him down. We didn't end on good terms."

"No offense, dear, but that sounds like a you problem, and you had better fix it before it becomes my problem. Otherwise, you will make a new enemy this night."

"I'll do what I can."

"Hurry," she replied. "I can only keep your attack silent for so long, and if you haven't fixed it by then, I fear you will be public enemy number one."

CHAPTER THIRTY-EIGHT

I opened a can of worms, kicked a hornet's nest, and whatever other crazy metaphor there was to explain being completely fucked. I went to Councilwoman Lane hoping for an ally in the fight against Black Jack, and she had thrown me to the wolves. *Ah, there's another one.*

The only person who knew where to find Dodo was Caterpillar, and if I showed up in front of him again, he would expect me to have made progress with the case, and as far as I knew, he was the one responsible for William's death.

In retrospect, it made complete sense. He had no allegiance to William, and if he could use him as a pawn to start a war with a rival, that's what he would do. After all, William was an agent of the White Queen. It wouldn't surprise me if he decided to keep him close to extract as much information as possible and then dispose of him when there was no value left inside of him.

At least I had a whole subway ride to get a lie together before I showed up at the Looking Glass Lounge. Most of the metro agents were off at night, and there was very little protection on the train when you hopped on it after midnight. As a woman, I was targeted more than most, so I had to keep my head on a swivel as I sat at the front of the train car, nearest the door, in case I needed a quick escape.

As I watched people get on and off at one of the stops, my phone rang, and it was Arthur. Fuck. I told him I was going to sleep at his house tonight.

"Hey, babe," I replied, laying on a rare term of endearment to hopefully tamp his anger toward my late hour.

"So…are you coming?" he asked.

"The fact that you asked that means the papers haven't gotten the latest yet, then?"

"What does that mean?" His voice suddenly turned to one of concern. "Are you okay?"

"Absolutely not, but I will be. I think. It's a long story, and I will tell you all about it when I've fixed everything."

"And if you don't fix it?" he asked. "It's not like you have a great track record of fixing things."

"No, you're right. Breaking things is more my forte, but I'm trying, and I don't want to bring anyone else into it." *Anyone who I bring into it has done nothing but fuck me over anyway.* "Long story short, I might be there, but don't count on it. I'll call you when this is all over."

"I don't like it…" He sighed. " I should tell you that if you are on the run from something, and you have a cellphone, they can track you."

Shit. He was right. "Thank you."

"Get a burner and text me from it so at least I know you are okay."

"I don't want to get you involve—"

"I don't need to be involved. I just need to know I can text you if I haven't heard from you in a while. I won't tell it to anyone, and I won't bug you unless I haven't heard from you by tomorrow night, okay?"

I growled. "Fine."

Luckily, in Wonderland, all sorts of places were open late, and I was able to ditch my phone and get a burner at a bodega on the corner two blocks from the Looking Glass Lounge. When I unwrapped it and turned it on, I made one text to Arthur's number. *It's me.*

I didn't care much about my phone. It was a police issue and came with all sorts of restrictions about what apps I could download, and you couldn't even play games on it. It was completely useless, and when this was over, I could easily get another one. I honestly couldn't believe I didn't think to ditch my phone earlier. Arthur might be annoying, but he did save my ass on that one.

I rushed over the street and past the lion and bear guarding the door to the lounge. At this point, they knew me, and I wondered as I passed how many people they had killed in service to Caterpillar.

When I reached inside, the club was back to full force, with exotic dancers writhing on the many stages and dozens of patrons around the bars enjoying the show. Caterpillar seemed completely disinterested in the corner, and the tiger who killed William stood in front of him, protecting him from everything around the bar.

My body clenched as I walked toward him, knowing the man was a killer, but when Caterpillar saw me, he whistled loudly, and it cut through the tension.

"There yhou ahre," he groused. "I thought I whould fhind yhou in a ditch tomorrow."

"Is that a threat?" I asked.

"Nho, just a concerned employer whorried about his invhestment."

Worried? No, you used me as a way to create a gang war and then beat a rival. You weren't worried about me. You were worried your plan would fail.

"I'm fine," I replied.

"And what did yhou fhind out?" he asked. "Have yhou fhound poor Whilliam's khiller yhet?"

I wanted to tell him the truth, but I held it back. "I'm afraid my investigation is at an impasse. You might have heard what happened at the station today."

He nodded. "Yes, terrible business, that. It rheally puts a damper on our rhelationship."

"I have a plan, but I need to find Dodo."

"He has flowhn the coohp, I'm afhraid," Caterpillar said with a chuckle. He always thought he was so smart and clever. I couldn't wait to see the look on his face when it all blew up around him. "So sad."

"If you want my help," I said, "I need Dodo."

He picked at the table. "That is an interhesting turn of phrase, bhecause I have decidhed…I don't."

"Excuse me?" I replied.

"I dhon't need yhour help." He snapped his fingers. "Yhou ahre more trouble than yhou are worth."

"What?" I slammed my hands on the table. "What about being concerned about me?"

He scratched his chin. "Yes, whell it thurns out I whas more concerned yhou whould turn on me, and nhow I can make sure that doesn't happen." He smiled. "In retrhospect, I suppose that whas a threat afhter ahll."

The tiger turned and, in one motion, grabbed me around the chest and pulled me from my seat. I tried to use bodyweight to kick at him, but he simply gripped me tighter as a half-transitioned bull squeezed my legs and pulled me out of the bar. The patrons barely registered my struggling, and the dancers didn't stop writhing, even for a second, like it was the most normal thing in the world.

CHAPTER THIRTY-NINE

I really fucked myself this time. In trying to play both sides against the middle, I never thought it possible Caterpillar would grow less enamored with me and cast me out into the cold, black night, but that was exactly what happened. Except for the fact that when Caterpillar cast you out, he did it with extreme prejudice.

After being thrown into the back of an unmarked, nondescript black van by the bull and the tiger, they bound me tight with bungee cord and started off to the outskirts of town. I saw how the White Queen dealt with her problems, and it was clear Caterpillar had a similar idea when it came to that subject.

"Can you loosen these up a bit?" I asked the tiger, who had taken a seat beside me while the bull drove. "If I'm going to die, I'd at least like to be comfortable before you kill me."

The tiger chuckled. "Don't push your luck, or we'll kill you right here."

"I don't believe you. If you just tossed me in the trash, I would be found, and even though nobody likes me, they don't take kindly to killing a cop."

"We can kill you here and bury you in the desert."

"And get the smell of death all over your nice van? I don't think your boss would like that much."

"Gag her!" the bull growled.

"Wait!" I shouted as the tiger moved forward. "I'll be good, okay, but please, don't make me live the last hour of my life with a gag in my mouth."

The tiger looked at the bull, who shrugged. "Fine, but if you piss me off again, we'll gag you and knock you out for good measure. You'll wake up dead six feet under."

I wanted to explain that you couldn't wake up dead, but I honestly couldn't care less about the bull's use of semantics. "You're the boss."

"He's not the boss," the tiger said. "We're co-workers."

I felt resentment in the tiger's voice and thought that I might take advantage of any animosity they had between them. "Can I ask you a question, tiger man?"

"I would rather you shut up."

"I appreciate that, but—it's just—I have a question that is gnawing at me, and if I don't ask it before I die…"

The tiger sighed. "Ask away then, but remember you're on thin ice."

"Oh, I don't think there's any way for me not to remember that, friendo," I said with a smile. "So—" I took a deep breath. "When Caterpillar asked you to kill that punk kid from the White Queen's army, did you have any reservations with the fact that he was going to use his body to start a gang war, or were you cool with it?"

A look of panic washed over the tiger's face. "I don't— what are you talking about?"

"Don't worry. I'm not going to say anything, and I doubt he"—I pointed to the driver with a jerk of my head— "will say anything to anyone if he knows what's good for him. It's just if I were going to be responsible for igniting a war that could kill half the city, I would have some qualms about it."

"What is she talking about, Carl?" the bull said from the front. "Caterpillar's been furious about that kid's death for months. Is she saying you had something to do with it?"

Well, that was new information. I was just trying to get the bull jealous with Carl, the tiger, but now I was suspicious about whether Caterpillar even put out a hit on William in the first place.

"She's crazy!" Carl growled. "I'm gonna gag her!"

"Wait!" I shouted. "Are you saying Caterpillar didn't order the hit on that poor kid, bull-man?"

"It's Eddy, and he's been absolutely furious every day since that kid's death, saying it was going to ruin his reputation. Even in private, he couldn't get over it. I can't imagine he would act on the shitter, but I heard him screaming about it even in the bathroom."

"Interesting." I cocked my head at Carl. "So, were you working for somebody else then?"

"I'm not saying shit to you, narc!" Carl screamed.

He lunged at me, and I used my legs to kick him backward. "I know almost every criminal in this city, and weird as it might be, I have never met another morpher that could afford such an amazing job turning into a tiger. I've met some really shit jobs, sure, and some mediocre ones, but when I saw your face on that tape, I knew it could only be you."

"You're fucking racist, man!" Carl growled. "They could have brought anyone in to strangle that kid."

I didn't realize until Carl finished talking that we stopped on the side of the road. Eddy looked back at Carl with venom in his eyes. "Tell me the truth, brother. Did you kill that kid? 'Cuz if you did—"

"I didn't do shit! She's a fucking liar—" Carl drew a gun from a holster in his pocket, and a shot cracked through the car. My ears rang and my eyes squeezed tight, waiting for the sting of a bullet to graze me, but when I opened my eyes, I saw Carl dead on the other side of the car, bleeding from a wound in his head.

"I never liked that guy," Eddy said as he turned.

"Me either," I replied. "Thanks."

"Don't thank me," he replied. "I'm still going to kill you. This was just a twofer. Now, when I go back and tell the boss what happened to William, he'll think I'm a hero. Too bad I couldn't stop Carl before you killed him."

"Oh," I replied, deflated. "Great. I'm so happy for you."

CHAPTER FORTY

Well, shit. I got one of the bad guys to kill the other, but the one left still ended up driving me into a field and throwing me on the ground with a shovel. This was not going well. Of all the things that happened in the past few months, this might have been the worst. The fact that I couldn't be sure said more about me than I cared to admit.

"Dig," he growled at me, uncoupling the bungies that held me tight. "Now."

I got to my feet and looked down at the shovel. "You've gotta be kidding me. Do people actually agree to that shit?"

"Excuse me?" he shouted, shoving the barrel of a shotgun into my back. "Dig."

I twisted toward him, trying to get a better look at the gun. "You expect me to do your job for you? So the last hour of my life is meant to be spent doing manual labor for you? Are you out of your gods damned mind?"

"I said d—"

I spun around and grabbed the barrel of the gun, knocking Eddy the bull in the nose with my elbow, which stunned him enough for me to grab the gun and shove it away from him. I spun the handle and smacked him in the face with it, sending him to the ground, and then stood over him with the gun pointed at his crotch.

"That's not very nice, Eddy," I replied. "If you want to kill somebody, the least you can do is dig their fucking grave, you lazy sack of shit. Now, keys."

"You'll never get away with this," he said, digging his hands into his pockets. "I'll kill you."

"Better men than you have tried, and while they might still succeed, I don't have high hopes for you." My eyes narrowed. "Now, strip down to your underwear."

"You've gotta be kidding me."

"Do I look like I'm fucking kidding?" I shouted. He shook his head and went about undressing for me until he was down to his underwear. "Good boy."

"You're not gonna kill me now, are you?"

"No, Eddy. That would be a mercy." I took his clothes and threw them in the passenger seat of the car. "Before I leave your sorry ass here to walk home, tell me—how many idiots actually dig their own grave?"

"All of them," he replied.

"Fucking morons." I took the gun and clocked him in the jaw with it, knocking him out. That way, if somehow somebody found him on the road, at least it would buy me a couple of hours. "Now, it's time to unfuck my life."

I still wasn't sure how, but I was sick of this bullshit, and it ended tonight.

CHAPTER FORTY-ONE

Caterpillar wanted to kill me. Deedum wanted to manipulate me. Councilwoman Lane wanted me to be her errand girl. All three of them were powerful enough to make my life a living Hell for the foreseeable future. How do you circle a square like that when everyone wanted either your head or your hide?

Go on the offensive. I was a detective, so detect. There was only one person who could disrupt the bullshit flung at me from great heights: Dodo, and who knows where I would find him.

My only choice was to go to the places I knew he would be and work backward from there. People weren't usually as sneaky as they believed. Even the best of them had tells, comfortable spots they liked to lie low. It was a rare type who could completely cut ties with everything they once knew. I had come in contact with sociopaths like that, and they were often the types who got away with crimes because the human mind was meant to make the kinds of leaps they could. However, for the rest of humanity, there were always clues, and they usually came from other people.

Dodo didn't seem like a particularly social creature, but we all were to some degree. We all shouted out in the dark for somebody to hold in the cold, harsh reality of life. Even I needed other people, often to my detriment.

When I got out of the coffee shop at the place I dropped Dodo off, I thought about texting Arthur, but if somehow Caterpillar found out I texted him, then he would know I was still alive, and I wasn't ready for that yet.

The coffee shop was closed since it was the middle of the night, which of course, I should have known. I could have waited for it to open, but eventually, the bull and the tiger would be missed, and somebody would go looking for them. I needed to end this before Caterpillar found out I was alive and started a manhunt for me.

Instead of the coffee shop, I headed to Dodo's office, the one that burned down, to look for clues to his whereabouts. The fire department had long gone since I left the street, and all that remained was the charred husk of a triangular house and a bunch of wires connecting a metal pole that pointed to the sky.

I knelt and started to scrape through the debris. My hands were quickly covered with char, along with the knees of my pants, and all I found were some aluminum trays and the chassis of his computer, along with the monitors that cracked and curled in the fire.

"Aw, man. Dodo did it, huh? He finally did it." I turned around to see a boy with neon green tips, a dozen piercings on his face, including on each side of his lip and nose, along with clothes so baggy it was hard to tell anything about his body from the amorphous blob of felt he wore.

"Who are you?" I replied, narrowing my eyes.

"I'm no—" He took a step back. "You a cop? You look like a cop."

I stood and wiped myself off. "I don't know what I am anymore."

That wasn't a satisfying answer for the boy, and he took off running the other way. However, he didn't get far before tripping over his baggy pants. I rushed forward and latched onto him, grabbing him toward the car.

"Don't hurt me, man. I didn't do anything wrong."

I smelled the air. "I don't have to frisk you to know you're carrying. How much did you sell to Dodo? Tell me the truth, and I won't arrest you."

"Shit, shit, shit. I can't tell you that. He would kill me if—"

I didn't let him finish his sentence before my gun was at his temple. "And what do you think I'll do if you waste my time?"

"Y—y—you don't scare me," he stuttered, clearly scared. "I know you narcs don't shoot people."

I chuckled. "I don't know what kind of narcs you know, but the kind I know kill little shits like you all the time." I pulled back the hammer on my gun. "I can't say I enjoy it much, and I'll have to get my car detailed, but I know a guy who'll fix it right up. Now, talk."

"All right!" He flinched. "I sold him an eighth every other week, along with some uppers. Dude liked to stay up all night for days on end and then smoke enough to kill a whale to come down."

I pulled him tighter. "And he spoke about burning this place down often?"

"Pretty often. Every time he got a line of code wrong. I thought he was just kidding, but damn, man." He looked over at the wreckage. "I guess not."

"Focus on me," I replied, and his eyes found mine again. "Good. Now, did he say where he would go if he burned this place down?"

"He said lots of things, man. Bali, Fiji, literally any third-world country in the world. He always talked about not being found. Of course, that would be impossible."

"And why is that?"

"Dude loved the internet too much. He always laughed about how he had the best internet in the whole city. Anywhere he went, it would have to have slamming upload and download speeds. That dude was a fiend."

That's right. He told me how good his internet was when I went to his place. He said he had the fastest in the city and that he lived in the second-fastest spot for internet in the city. Suddenly, I knew what I had to do, but I wasn't going to like it.

"Get in," I shouted, opening the door. "And give me your phone."

CHAPTER FORTY-TWO

If I never had to run around Wonderland with a teenager in a van that wasn't mine, it would be too soon. Hopefully, this one didn't end up dead, though. I really didn't like the only plan I was able to come up with, but at least it only had a 90% chance of blowing up in my face, which, compared to my other options, was actually pretty good.

I grabbed a paper bag full of N'baka's favorite Indian food and handed it to the kid. "Tell them you're from Al Noor, and you have a delivery for N'baka in forensics. He'll be confused, but he's not going to deny food." I wrote a note on the napkin and folded it up inside. "Can you handle that?"

He raised his eyebrows. "You want me to walk into the lion's den with food and offer myself up as a sacrifice, ay? And what's in it for me?"

I held up the drugs I pulled off him at a traffic light. "I won't turn you in for this."

"Lady, you can't even go into your old precinct, but I'm pretty amped to see how this turns out, so I'll play along. If I get caught, though, I'm going to sing like a canary. I'll tell you that right now."

"Then don't get caught, for both of our sakes. Make it back here, and you get the money."

"A grand, right?" he asked.

"That's right."

"Lady, you are desperate. It's my favorite scent on a woman."

He hopped out of the van and slid the side door closed. He took a second to get his bearings and then strutted to the front door. It wasn't long until he was inside, his body lit by the fluorescent lights inside. This was the hardest part because he could turn on me at any second. He didn't, though. Either it was the money, or the simple intrigue of it, that made him keep up the ruse, and in five minutes, N'baka was upstairs, very confused, taking possession of a big bag of food.

He was meticulous when eating, laying out everything on his table and cleaning every plastic container before it touched his pristine table. It was annoying as all hell to watch, but in this circumstance, I hoped it meant he would find my note and meet me without alerting the narcs. This was the second most dangerous part of the plan because he could give the bag to somebody, miss the note, or find it and turn it in. I was taking it on a lot of faith that he wasn't on the take. After all, I thought Dormouse would never turn and look at what happened to him.

"I should have asked you to get me some," the kid said when he got back to the van. "Now, where's the money?"

"When my friend shows up, you'll get your money."

"That wasn't part of the deal," he scoffed.

"Well, I'm changing the deal." I turned around, hand on my holster. "Do you have a problem with that?"

"Fuck yes, I have a problem with that," he growled, taking no notice of the position of my hand, or if he noticed it, he didn't pay it any mind. "You're gonna fuck me, aren't you?"

"Absolutely am not going to fuck you."

He put his hands behind his head. "Not that I would mind. I mean, I don't know if that ass is worth a grand, but I'm willing to make a real nice deal for it."

"I would pay double never to have to touch you again," I replied. "But don't worry. You'll get your money, but not if I get arrested."

"I got that much," he replied. "Don't worry. That guy seemed cool."

"He's one of the good ones," I replied. "Maybe too good to help me."

That was something I hadn't considered. Maybe he would just burn the note and go about his life like I never existed. After all, he had a family to protect, and who was I? Some low-life, corrupt, drug-addled cop. Why would he put his career on the line for me? Would I do the same for him? Would I do the same for anyone anymore? *Doubtful.*

But then again, I wasn't a good person. I wasn't much of a person at all, actually, let alone a good one. Most days, I felt like a monkey, dancing for pennies on a street corner, beset in every direction by people who wanted to trample me, and held tight by people more powerful than me, willing to make their bones off my work without ever lifting a finger themselves.

"There he is!" the kid said, pointing to an alley next to the station. N'baka must have been a way better person than me, even if it took him forty minutes to come find me.

He crossed the street and scanned the horizon. When he found the van, he scuffled to it. I rolled down my window and smiled at him. "You ate first, didn't you?"

"Of course, I ate first," N'baka said, holding up a sheet of paper. "For what you asked, it was the least you could do to wait for me."

"I'm not good at waiting, friendo." I took the sheet of paper. "Thank you for this."

"You're welcome. Now go; they are on high alert for you. I don't have to tell you the pee they tested showed you were pregnant. So, live through the night so you can see that baby born."

"I'm not—" I sighed. I wasn't about to tell him everything. It would take too long. "Thank you for that, too. I'll be careful."

"Bullshit," N'baka said. "But it's a nice lie, so I'll allow it."

CHAPTER FORTY-THREE

I asked N'baka to triangulate the best locations for internet connection in the city, and boy did he deliver. He handed me a map with handwritten cross-streets for the top five places that had the fastest internet speed in the city. The first place we already knew, and N'baka's map confirmed it. The second was an office building downtown constructed in the 1800s.

"I heard of that place," the kid in the back said, looking over my shoulder. "Dodo told me it was constructed from some material they didn't know was hyper-conductive for internet or something like that."

I was sure Dodo said it more coherently than that, but I got the gist, and we headed to the Rampant building, about fifteen blocks from Black Jack Security. As we moved through the city, I got the eerier suspicion we were being followed, and when I looked behind, I found a black town car driving with no lights on. I took the next right and then two more left before taking a U-turn back to where I was going.

When I looked back in the mirror, my breath came back to me, but then the light shifted, and I saw the black car again. My heart thumped in my chest. It could have been anyone following me, from any of the many people trying to track me down or somebody I didn't even know about. Maybe the White Queen wasn't Mr. Deedum, and they were finally in on the chase to bring me down.

I pulled the van over two blocks from the Rampant building and pulled the kid out of the car. "Let's go."

"I don't have a good feeling about this."

"Well, aren't you the genius?"

I pushed him into the darkness as I waited for the car to pull over. Sure, enough. Two men with black suits stepped out of the vehicle and examined the open van. When they went to call their boss, I went to attack.

"Yeah, bo—" One of them started into a cell phone, and I went for their legs. I was able to kick one of their feet out from under them. They flipped into the air, and I caught the phone they dropped.

Before the other had a chance to react, I pulled the gun from its holster and smashed him across the nose with it, pushing him over the car as the first guy rose. He swung, and I ducked, using their momentum against them to smash them into the van door as hard as I could and then flinging them into their partner until they both tumbled over.

"Who is this?" I growled into the phone. I didn't need them to know about each other. I would make them come to me. Or I would have if they didn't hang up.

With them down, I stepped over to the guys and looked over their writhing bodies. One of them pointed to me. "You need to end this."

"Who do you work for?" I asked, not expecting an answer. When I didn't get one, I turned to walk away. "Tell them to fuck off, or I won't be so polite next time."

I scrolled through the phone quickly but didn't see a number I recognized or a name, and the one they called was simply labeled as "boss." Maybe I should have kept the phone, but then maybe it could be tracked, so I left it with the guards and walked off with the kid.

"What is your name anyway?" I asked.

"They call me Gryphon."

"But that's not your name?" I asked.

"It's not *not* my name, if you know what I mean. It's not on my birth certificate, though. I hate that name. I used to get made fun of mercifully for it. I figure if people can morph into new animals, I can at least change my name."

"That's okay, kid. I don't need to deadname you. Gryphon is fine by me. My name is Alice."

"Oh shit," he said, laughing. "Are you that detective that shot—" He must have seen my eyes because he stopped talking. "Sorry. It's just—you're a legend."

I sighed. "Yeah, well…not in a good way."

"Who cares?" he replied. "I'm trying to make a name for myself any way I can, and you did it, even if it's not in the best way."

"You say that now, kid, but what is that thing Bill Murray says? If you think being rich and famous will solve all your problems, try being rich first and see if that doesn't fix most everything. I got all the shitty parts of fame with none of the riches. It's not all it's cracked up to be."

"Bullshit. People know you by just your face."

"They make opinions about me behind my back. Do you have any idea what it's like to have people hate you who know nothing about you? What about millions of people? I got judged for the worst three seconds of my life. How would you like to be known for the worst thing you ever did?"

He sucked his teeth. "When you say it like that, it does kind of feel like shit. But you gotta be able to parlay that shit into endorsement deals or something. I mean, fame is fame."

I chuckled. "Who do you think would want me as a spokesperson?"

"I dunno. There's gotta be some racist twats who sell guns or some shit."

"Pass." I looked up at an old art deco building collapsing to a point high above me. There was a big chrome sign that said "Rampant" in blocky letters. "I think this is the place."

"What gave you that idea?" Gryphon said.

"Oh." I shrugged. "Just a NARCO's instincts, I guess."

CHAPTER FORTY-FOUR

Even though it was the dead of night, the doors to the Rampart building were open. We walked up to a security guard dressed in a gray jumper and sweating profusely while trying to maintain a pained smile.

"How—how can I help you?" she asked. After a second, she flinched as if somebody had just yelled at her.

"Are you okay, dude?" Gryphon asked. "You look like death."

The woman quivered for a long moment and then stood straighter. "I'm fine, sir. How can I help you?"

"We're looking for a man calling himself Dodo. Do you know him?"

A hint of recognition passed her eyes, and then she blinked. "I've never—and why do you want to see him?"

"FUCKING SHIT, Susan!" the intercom screeched in a familiar voice. "You are the worst actor in the history of the fucking universe!"

"Dodo?" I asked, confused. "Is that you?"

"Yeah, it's me," Dodo growled. "The fuck do you want?"

"I ca—" I didn't want to yell it. "Can we come talk to you?"

"Are you kidding me?" he shouted. "What if you're trying to kill me?"

"I don't think she is, mate," Gryphon said. "I've been around her all night, and she's been nothing but straight with me. Even gave me a grand for doing a really basic ass errand.”

“Huh—Gryphon? Is that you, dude? Holy shit. What are you doing here?”

“Well, I was looking to sell you your monthly eighth, and this random bitch was sifting through the rubble of your old house. One thing led to another, and here we are.”

“Don’t call me a bitch,” I snapped at Gryphon.

“You are a bitch!” he shouted. “I’m in all of this hot mess because of you.”

There was a long silence, and then the intercom screeched to life. “Susan, let them up! Then, give them your keys, and you can go. If you can’t play the part, what fucking good are you?”

The woman nodded and handed us the keys. Then she pushed some buttons, and the elevator door opened. “It’s really easy. Thirtieth floor. The elevator would take you right there, but honestly, I’d go if I were you. He’s fucking crazy.”

“I heard that, Susan!” he shouted. “Get the fuck out of here.”

“Good luck!” Susan didn’t wait another second to bolt out of the door.

We walked to the elevator, but the intercom screeched to life. “Not yet. Go to the door and pull the security doors, then you can come up.”

I rolled my eyes, but I needed him alive and happy, so I walked to the front door and found a gate that pulled down to barricade the windows. I found a lock in the floor and locked them into place, all around the glass entrance, until we were sealed in. For some odd reason, I felt safe for the first time all night.

Then Gryphon and I walked to the elevator. This time the intercom didn't screech, and when we walked inside, the doors closed behind us. Right before they did, all the lights in the lobby turned off at once, and I got a sinking feeling in the pit of my stomach that something was wrong.

"We're gonna die, huh?" Gryphon said, with only a minimum of regret in his voice. "That kind of sucks."

"I already almost died today. This won't be the second time somebody tried to kill me if it happens. I have a habit of surviving these things."

"And what about the people with you?"

I stopped for a moment. "Their odds are lower."

"Awesome."

When the elevator doors opened, a panicked Dodo paced back and forth, biting his fingernails. "You really fucked me, Detective. You right FUCKED me. Did you know that?"

"I didn't—I'm sorry? Also, how?"

"I have been fighting attacks all day. I finally had to take my server offline, which means I can't do any-fucking-thing online. These fuckers are good, but so far, I've been better. I've been trying to reset myself on an external server, but I don't trust anyone out there. It fucking sucks. Do you know how much money I lost today because of you?"

"I don't—a couple thousand?"

He chuckled. "Try three million. That's on your ass."

"Three million dollars!" Gryphon shouted. "Holy fuck. I knew you were loaded, but holy fuck."

"How the hell do you make that kind of money? You're like twelve."

"Ever hear of crypto? I started mining Bitcoin early and Ethereum even earlier. It's the fucking wild west, and you can literally destroy countries or mint millionaires if you know what you're doing. It's a fucking scam, but a great one." His eyes narrowed at me. "But don't change the subject. I'm pissed at you."

"I really am sorry. I knew Black Jack was filled with petty fucks, but I really didn't want to ruin your life."

"Women never do." He sighed. "Come with me. You need to see this."

"What?" I asked.

"The video that's going to get us all killed tonight."

CHAPTER FORTY-FIVE

Dodo's office wasn't much of one. It was more like an elaborate gamer's wet dream, with several dozen consoles set up around with cushy couches and trays for snacking, and there were half-eaten bags of chips and opened soda cans on each of them. It looked like he hadn't cleaned in days, if not weeks.

"I'm sorry for the mess. Usually, the maids come in every night, but I paid them to take the month off just in case…"

I waited for him to finish, but when he didn't, I stepped toward him. "In case of what? You sound like you're preparing for a war."

"Oh, I'm absolutely preparing for a war." He pointed to the ceiling, where video cameras were aimed at the door, armed with machine guns underneath them. "If you had tried to come in without my permission, I would have blown you halfway to kingdom come."

"I'm glad you didn't," Gryphon said. "This is a sick setup, man. We should have a kickback, invite some friends, and I'll get us all ripped."

Dodo stopped and smiled. "I…have never had anyone inside this place before. That would be nice."

I got the feeling that Dodo didn't have many, if any, friends outside of Gryphon, and he was only there because he was paid for the privilege. Underneath the steely-eyed demeanor, Dodo was still a scared kid, barely old enough to be out on his own.

"You should come, beautiful," Gryphon said with a wink. He was a cocky little shit for somebody I could absolutely destroy with one punch to the throat.

"Call me beautiful again, and I'll throw you out that window."

"Oh, you can't do that," Dodo said. "I paid to have tempered glass installed when I moved in. Nothing is getting through that short of a fucking assault helicopter."

"You're paranoid, Dodo," I said, marveling at the level of protection he had for himself. "I like that about you."

Dodo smiled as if nobody had ever given him a compliment before. "I hate you, but thank you for that."

"Oh, I don't like you, either. Don't get it twisted. I just like a man who knows how to take care of himself."

"I can take care of myself," Gryphon said with a smarmy growl and raised eyebrows. "I'm just saying."

I rolled my eyes and continued through the office until we reached the far side, where a massive monitor bank rested at the corner of two windows and dwarfed the one from the small house that was Dodo's old base of operations. The monitors were playing porn as we walked up, and Dodo barely took notice of the two men railing a black woman as he sat down and swiped it away.

"Before I show this to you," Dodo said as he typed on his computer, "I should come clean with you."

"That would be nice," I replied.

"I made a backup of the information we took from Black Jack Security. It was right there, and I couldn't resist."

"I'm not surprised. You are a criminal after all."

He shook his head. "I wish I didn't, really I do."

My eyes narrowed, and I realized something. "This has to do with more than just taking the data, doesn't it? You found something in those files."

He sighed. "My curiosity got the better of me, so I started going through everything we got, trying to figure out what was so important they would track me so hard. That's when I found this video, and everything became clear to me. This is the point where you close your eyes and cover your ears because the minute you see this video, the forces of Hell won't stop until they kill you."

I looked over at Gryphon, wondering if he would close his eyes, but his curiosity got the best of him, just like it had me. Dodo gave us a second more to change our minds, but when we didn't, he listed his head back to the monitor and hit play.

A grainy video popped onto the monitor. Even in the pixelated black and white, I could make out Councilwoman Lane standing inside an elevator. The elevator stopped on a floor, and Jack Fowler walked inside. The doors closed, and he slammed the emergency button, stopping it in its tracks.

"A weird place to want to meet," Councilwoman Lane said. "This better be good. I'm not going to change my mind about running."

Jack Fowler chuckled. "This isn't about that, Councilor. I called you here because I know what you're planning."

"Wiping the Roses off the map and taking control of the city council? That's not hard to figure out."

"No," Jack said. "I know you plan on taking over the White Rabbit trade for yourself, using a pseudonym called the White Queen."

"What?" The councilwoman scoffed. "That's ridiculous."

Jack Fowler took a folder from inside his coat and handed it to her. "Is it? These documents show otherwise, and I'm ready to go to the police if you don't give me what I want."

Councilwoman Lane's face tightened into a vengeful stare. "And what do you want? Me to leave the city council? To disappear and never be heard from again?"

"Nothing so grand as that. I want in. Fifty percent of the take, and I'll provide muscle so loyal you'll never have to worry about them turning on you."

"Yeah, but will you turn on me?" the councilwoman said. "How do I know you are loyal?"

Jack Fowler crossed his hands. "We both have images to maintain, and I have no desire to go to jail, but more importantly, I went to Caterpillar with a similar proposal, and he turned me away. I want to watch him twist in the wind. I'll be loyal to you as long as you help me bury him."

She chuckled. "That is something I can absolutely guarantee."

"Then we have an agreement?"

She nodded. "We are agreed, but if you fuck me over—"

"Oh, trust me, Councilor. If I ever fuck you, it won't be over, and you'll enjoy it more than when you get it from that cowardly husband you have." She tried to hand the paper over to him. "Keep it. I have plenty more."

"We won't be able to meet, except in secret," she said.

He nodded. "I have it all worked out. This meeting is going to have gone badly, and you'll sue me. I'll *countersue, giving us plenty of reasons to meet together, but on the opposite sides of the law. Eventually, when they buy it, we'll settle for the first part of my cut, and everyone will believe we hate each other."*

She nodded. "I have to admit, that's a pretty good plan. I didn't think you had it in you."

He slammed the button, and the elevator started again. "Oh, you have no idea what I have in me, Councilor."

With that, the video went black, and I stared at the screen, slack-jawed. The councilwoman was the White Queen this whole time? How had I not seen it? How had she kept it secret this long? How did I have such terrible taste in people?

"Aw, shit, man," Gryphon said. "I really wish you hadn't shown me that." I felt a tug on my hip, and when I turned, Gryphon had my gun in his hands. "Why did you have to find that stupid tape?"

CHAPTER FORTY-SIX

"What the hell are you doing?" Dodo asked Gryphon as he spun in his chair.

"Don't fucking move, either of you!" Gryphon growled. "I will fucking kill you. I don't want to kill you, but it's too much money. I'll fucking kill you if I have to."

"What do you mean 'too much money,' Gryphon?" I asked as I held up my hands. You had to talk calmly to people holding guns, so they didn't get excited and pull the trigger. Even if you wanted nothing more than to punch them right in the face, you had to wait for your shot.

"The White Queen. She put out a call for Dodo. I didn't want to—but she offered ten million dollars. It's so much fucking money, man. That kind of money, I could be set for life."

"So you'd just turn on me, you little shit?" Dodo said, staying pretty calm for the little I knew about him. I was trained in dealing with psychos who stole your gun, but he was keeping a more level head than I thought he could.

"Turn on you? We're not friends, man. I sell you weed. Just because you're a pathetic little pussy with no friends isn't my problem. Now just shut up. This will all be over soon." He turned to me. "Hand me my phone."

"I can't do that, Gryphon."

He shook the gun at me. "I will fucking kill you, bitch, and take the phone off your bullet-riddled corpse."

"I don't know about that, Gryphon. It's pretty hard to kill a person. I did it once, and it fucked me up for a long time. I haven't even been able to hit the broad side of a barn since then."

"Are you kidding me? You held a gun to my head to get me to help you!"

"I'm a pretty good liar. I was on Caterpillar's payroll for months, and nobody found out. It got me very good at deception. Now, put down the gun, and we can talk about this. Nobody has to find out."

"Yeah, dude," Dodo said. "If it means that much to you, I will wire you ten million fucking dollars."

"Shut up, asshole," he said. "You're not that rich. Don't even play."

"You have no idea how early I got into Bitcoin," Dodo said. "If you let me go to my computer, I will show you."

"Don't fucking move!" Gryphon said as Dodo went to spin around. "I know the kind of shit you can do with that monitor." He turned back to me. "And give me that fucking phone!"

I didn't have any other choice except a bold one. "Okay, I'm reaching into my pocket. Don't shoot me."

"Slowly, bitch."

I lowered my hand slowly into my pocket and found the phone. I pulled it out and lobbed it to him. For a moment, Gryphon's eyes stopped looking at me to find the phone, and I used that moment to charge and smash him into the windows. I socked him in the gut and then hit him in the face when he dropped his guard. He let out a soft sigh as he fell to the floor, unconscious.

I grabbed the phone and put it back in my pocket, and turned to Dodo. "We have to get out of here."

"Are you fucking crazy?" he said. "This place is locked up tighter than a dolphin's asshole."

"Then we have to get that information somewhere. Once it's out, then they will go down, but while that information is a secret, we're sitting ducks."

Dodo started typing. "Why do you think I let you up here? I can't get back online without them finding my location, but you can get out and bring this to the masses." He pulled a flash drive out of a desk drawer and plugged it into the front of his computer. After a few seconds, the file finished copying and he pulled it out of the chassis. "Upload it to YouTube, whatever, and get it to the press. Otherwise, we are so fucked."

I grabbed the hard drive from him. "I'll do my best."

"Do better than that." He looked me up and down. "Also, you look like shit. Take a shower."

"When I can, but not while everyone is trying to kill me." I looked over at Gryphon. "What about him?"

"I'll figure out what to do with him. Just go."

"You don't have to tell me twice."

"I can't believe that I'm trusting a narc with my life."

"Then how about a friend?" I couldn't say it with a straight face before busting out laughing. "Sorry, I tried."

"Just get the fuck out of here!" Dodo growled. "God, I almost prefer death to your company."

"Same," I replied. "But let's not die tonight."

"That would be nice."

CHAPTER FORTY-SEVEN

I didn't want to disturb Arthur until I had this all figured out and the heat died down, but there was no denying that he was a reporter who could get this information into the right hands, which meant I had no other choice. It was him, or somebody I trusted even less than him.

So, I texted him; *I'm coming over. What's your address?*

When he finally texted back, I was at the bottom of the elevator. I knew the address, but it was halfway across town, which meant I needed to get to the subway. I didn't want to get back to the van because who knew what those two assholes who I knocked out cold were doing with it now.

"Wait!" the intercom blared when I was in the lobby. "Stay there."

I waited for Dodo to come down the elevator. He handed me my gun. "You forgot this."

I shook my head and put it in my holster. "Today has not been my best."

"Well, I forgot that I need to let you out of the door and take the key. Otherwise, I'll be a sitting duck. So, this whole thing has frazzled us both."

We walked to the door, and I unlocked one of the gates. "What are you going to do tomorrow morning when people want to come to work?"

"Fuck 'em," he replied with a smile.

However, his smile didn't last as two bullets fired into the lobby, and one of them bored deep into his stomach.

"Shit!" I shouted as more bullets rained down on us. "Get to cover!"

I pulled Dodo through the lobby and behind the security desk as the bullets shot around us. When we were safe behind the desk, Dodo looked down at his stomach, trying to dab out the blood. "Oh shit. I'm going to die. I'm going to die."

"You're not going to die. We need to get out of here to the hospital."

"No, no, no, no, no. I can't go outside. I can't. They are literally trying to kill me."

"And if you don't get that wound tended to, they're going to succeed. Do you have a car?"

He nodded. "Down in the basement. Level two."

"Then that's where we are going."

The baddies were tucked in the distance, and I laid down some suppressing fire as I dragged him to the still open elevator. When I went to get the button, the bullets flooded in again, peppering the door as it closed with me hidden behind it.

"What kind of car do you have?"

"It's a Tesla Model S. The nice kind. I'm on the waiting list for the Roadster. Ah shit. I'm going to bleed all over it."

The door opened, and I helped Dodo to his car. The blood trailed behind us, and we weren't hard to track. I laid him in the passenger seat and turned the car on. It had a nearly silent purr to it as I pushed the ignition and slammed it into drive.

"When we get to the hospital, they are going to have to call in your bullet wound. So keep—"

"No…" he said. "I know a guy."

"You know a bullet guy?" I sighed. "Of course, you do. You're a criminal."

I turned the car to the gated exit of the facility to find four men waiting outside with assault rifles trained on us. When I tried to turn around, I found three more waiting behind us. They must have come down the elevator.

"Give up!" one of them shouted.

"I don't think that's happening." I looked over at Dodo. "I'm sorry about this."

I revved the car into gear and shot it forward. The barrier had barely opened for us when we crashed into it, scraping the metal against his pretty hood. The men scrambled out of the way, and I swerved to avoid a big van waiting at the top of the gate. I smashed into the side of it but managed to right myself and slam the gas again as bullets peppered the car.

The men rushed for the van to chase us, but it was no match for the Tesla. It might have been an all-electric car, but it sped up like a dream.

"Don't die on me, okay?" I said as I swerved between cars.

"I'm not planning on it," he whispered. "Are you going to betray me, too?"

"What?" I replied. "I literally just saved your life. I could have left you back there, but I didn't."

"Fair," he replied. "Still…I don't have many people I can rely on. Nobody really."

I sighed. "I was going to turn you over to Councilwoman Lane so she would help me survive, but now I have a feeling she's not too eager to help me, so you're safe. Just tell me where we're going, and don't fall asleep."

He chuckled, causing him to wince. "I'm on so much Adderall I couldn't sleep if I tried."

CHAPTER FORTY-EIGHT

"Seriously?" I asked, pulling up to the North Wonderland Veterinary Clinic. "This is the place?"

"Don't knock it," Dodo replied. "Vets have to be able to work with all sorts of animals, including ones with bullet holes in them, and I am an animal with a bullet wound."

"Whatever, don't die in there. I'll check on you later."

He shook his head. "No, please don't leave. This is going to suck, and I need somebody to be there with me."

"Call your mom or somebody."

"Really? Would you call your mother if you got shot? What if those jerks show up? What if he leaves me for dead to collect on the reward? Come on, Alice. Have some heart."

"Fine," I growled. "But this better be quick. It's almost morning."

The sky had moved from a perfect amber to a dark blue in the hours I had been trying to clear myself, and while I needed to work fast, I couldn't let him fend for himself. I helped Dodo out of the car and around to the back of the clinic. He buzzed a number and said a code before the gate to the building swung open.

A thin, perfectly dressed man met us at the door and guided us into one of the rooms. "Hop up on the exam table."

There were pictures of puppies and kittens all over the hallways leading into the room and even more in the exam room. Dodo hopped up onto the table and lay down. "How bad is it, Doc?"

"Well," the vet said. "You got shot, but it doesn't look like it hit any major organs. I'll just go get my tools and—"

"I don't think so, Doc," I said. "Nobody leaves this room without guidance."

"I mean, you can come with me, but I think you're being paranoid."

"You're a vet who works with criminals and was still at work in the wee hours of the morning. That's sketchy as fuck, so yeah, I think I'll come with you."

The vet led me into the back of the building, where he disinfected his arms and gathered a collection of devices. "How did he get shot, if you don't mind me asking?"

"He was picking flowers. What does it matter to you?"

"Just making idle chit-chat. I see you're not the chatting type."

"Not usually, and even less so right now."

"Then let's get down to work."

We walked back to the room, and he pulled a vial of liquid from the kit he prepared. He walked over across the room and found a needle. "This is going to hurt a lot, so I'm going to numb the area first."

The doctor worked, injecting the liquid around the wound and disinfecting it with alcohol. When Dodo was numb, he began to work.

"I can't watch," Dodo said, turning to me.

"I can't either." I squeezed his hand hard, and he returned my viselike grip with one of his own. When the doctor started, Dodo tensed up completely, then relaxed after a few minutes when we heard a metal ting. I looked over to see the bullet resting in a metal bowl on the table.

"Now, I just have to sew it back up. You're lucky it was a clean wound."

"Nothing about this is lucky, Doc," Dodo said.

"You could have severed your spine, so I think that's pretty lucky."

"I guess that's true," I said.

After sewing Dodo up, we ambled to the front of the building. The bright lights of morning were starting to seep through the windows. Dodo paid the $25,000 fee with a credit card. I found it exorbitant, but Dodo assured me it was worth it to keep his lips shut, and we were gone in less than an hour.

"You'll need to find a medical doctor to check on you in a couple of days to make sure the stitches don't pop," the vet said when he opened the door for us. "And take it easy."

"I wish we could do that, Doctor."

I laid Dodo gingerly in the passenger's seat and then started the car again. He bitched and moaned about how I destroyed his car, but not once did he thank me for saving his life…of course, I was also the one who put it in danger, so maybe we were par for the course.

It didn't take more than ten minutes to make it across the rest of the city to Arthur's house, and when we arrived, I turned to him. "Wait in the car and rest. I will be out for you soon."

"Maybe I'll just leave."

"And go where?" I asked. "Once I know it's okay, I'll let you rest up at Arthur's place, assuming he's cool with it."

"If he's not?" Dodo asked.

"He will be," I replied. "I can be very persuasive."

He chuckled, again causing him to wince. "You're going to sex him, aren't you?"

"If that's what it takes," I replied. "I don't feel very sexy right now, though."

"You're crazy." He leaned back. "You're sexy as hell, girl."

I opened the door. "Never say that to me again, but thanks."

CHAPTER FORTY-NINE

I rang the doorbell, and Arthur came to get me. "Wow, you look terrible."

I pushed in past him. "Really? I thought I looked sexy."

Arthur's brownstone was filled with hundreds of pictures on the wall at every turn; of him with cute girls and tiny children; with old people, and a dozen men on a river. There were pictures of him in suits and in swim trunks. There was almost no room on any of the walls after accounting for all the pictures.

"Wow, you really love yourself, huh?" I said, hobbling into the kitchen and taking a seat on a barstool next to the counter. "Do you have any coffee? I didn't sleep last night, and I'm starting to feel it."

The adrenaline and fury carried me through the dark of night, but in the cold light of day, there was only so much I could do to keep up my energy without stimulants.

"Of course," he said, kissing me on the cheek. "It's nice to see you, too."

"Yes, it's nice to see you, Arthur, but I've had a shit night, and I need to tell you all about it, but I can't do it without coffee."

"I'm going," he said, walking to the coffee pot and filling it with water. "Does it have something to do with that Tesla outside that looked a hundred different types of fucked up? Because I would very much like to hear that story."

"I'm sure you would, and I'm going to tell it, but first coffee."

Arthur didn't ask me more questions before the coffee started to percolate, and he poured me a cup. "Do you want cream or sugar?"

"How long have we been fucking, Arthur? You know I take it black." I snatched the coffee from him and took a sip, realizing then that I was being a real bitch. "Sorry, it's just been a hell of a night."

"Well, I'm ready to hear all about it."

And so I told him everything, from nearly getting killed to stealing a van and from Dodo's office all the way to the veterinarian's office. When the coffee was done, I asked for more and finished two full pots by the time I finished my story.

"Wow," he said when I was finished. He was clearly a good reporter because he knew how to get me to talk and keep me talking with a minimum of interruptions. "That's quite a story. I feel like if I wrote a book about it, nobody would believe it."

I pulled out the flash drive and placed it on the table. "Nobody would believe half the crazy shit I get up to."

"Is that it?"

I nodded. "That's your Pulitzer, but you have to share it soon, like today. How long will it take you to get a story out?"

"Whoa, whoa, whoa," he replied. "This has to go through a whole bunch of channels and then be disseminated. It could take hours or days—"

"Days!" I shouted, grabbing the drive and walking toward the door. "I don't have that kind of time. They're after me, Arthur, and they're going to find me if we don't share this now."

Arthur grabbed me by the arm and twisted me around. "All right, all right. I'll see what I can do."

"I'll just put it on YouTube, Arthur. I need your help, but if it takes me talking to every person in Wonderland one at a time to make this thing go viral, I'll fucking do it."

He held up his hands. "Just let me look at it, okay? If it's as explosive as you say, then, of course, I'll get this fast-tracked, and we can protect you."

"Fuck that. Nobody can protect me from Councilwoman Lane. Nothing but the truth."

He held out his hand for the drive. "Just let me look at it. In the meantime, take a shower. I'm assuming you don't have clothes so just leave yours out and I'll put them in the wash, okay?"

I nodded and placed the drive in his hand. "I can trust you, can't I?"

"Of course."

I growled, relinquishing my claim on the drive to him. "That's what they all say. Where is your shower?"

"Upstairs, first door on the left."

I nodded. "When I come down, we need to talk about Dodo. He's in the car, and he really needs a place to rest."

"You can call me Hotel Arthur. Your friend is welcome to stay here."

"He's not my friend, but he's a witness to corroborate my story."

"I'll go bring him inside, okay?"

I allowed him to leave and watched him pull Dodo out of the car before I went upstairs, taking the stairs slowly as I looked at all the pictures lining them. He was so popular in a way I could never be and never wanted to be. It was no wonder he was such a popular reporter. He seemed to know everyone.

Then, I saw something that made me stop dead. A photo with Arthur and a much younger Councilwoman Lane, signed with the inscription: *To my first press secretary, May your new life be even more bountiful than this one. You're the best, Suzanne.*

Shit. He knew the councilwoman. Even worse, he was there when she started working with Black Jack Security. And I left the drive in his hands.

What have I done?

CHAPTER FIFTY

I pulled the gun out of its holster and eased down the stairs, watching for Arthur as I stepped gingerly to prevent them from hearing my footsteps.

"I'll come back to check on you in a minute," Arthur said from the front of the house. I tiptoed up the stairs as I watched him come toward me, but then he took a right down the hallway, holding the thumb drive in his hand.

I stepped down the stairs and followed behind him slowly, hugging the wall as he turned into a room down the hall. I stepped slowly and carefully as I heard a monitor turn on and the typing of a computer.

"What is on this drive then?" he muttered to himself as the mouse clicked. The video started, and I heard Councilwoman Lane first and Jack Fowler second. They spoke, just as they had previously when I listened, but it was even more incriminating the second time around. When it was done, he sighed and picked up the phone.

"We have it," he said. "No, she's upstairs showering. Okay."

My heart cracked open a little bit as I hoped for once I picked a guy that was good for me, but like everyone else, he was corrupt. I waited until he was done on the phone and then stepped into the room.

"Hi, darling."

"Alice!" he said, trying to crack a soft smile. "How long have you been there?"

"Long enough." I raised my gun. "Give me the thumb drive."

"What are you doing, Alice? I'm trying to help, and you're holding a gun to my head."

"Who were you talking to, Arthur?" I replied. "Councilwoman Lane, maybe? I saw how buddy-buddy you were in that picture."

"Shit," he replied, shaking his head.

"Your vanity will get you every time, Arthur. To think, you might have gotten away with it if you just could keep your pictures in a photo album like a normal person."

"You don't understand, Alice," Arthur said, standing up. "Who do you think scheduled those meetings between Jack and Samantha, huh? Do you have any idea how much shit she has on me? If I don't help her, I'll go down for it. She'll pin it on me and walk away scot-free."

"Give me the drive, Arthur, or I'll shoot you in the fucking head."

"I don't think you will." He reached into his pocket and produced a tape recorder. He played it, and my whole confession sang through the house. "It doesn't have to be this way. Let me end this, and we can both walk away."

"You think I believe that?"

"It's true," he replied. "We already got into Dodo's office. Took a couple of casualties with it, but we have the server, and this thumb drive is the last piece of the puzzle."

"Yeah, right. We are the last piece of the puzzle. Dodo and I. We saw the file, along with Gryphon. If we don't die, then there will always be the chance we talked."

"Well, Dodo will have to die, that's true, and we already took care of Gryphon. You're a foot soldier, though, Alice, and the councilor knows that. She also knows Caterpillar wants you dead and knows you've confessed to it. She has enough leverage to keep you in line. Plus, she owes me a few thousand favors for preventing this from coming out." He walked forward. "We can be happy, or you can be dead."

"Okay, Arthur." I dropped my eyes. "I have one question for you, though. How did those men know where I was this evening? Were you tracking my phone?"

He winced. "I'm sorry about that, but your police-issued one had too much security for us to crack. Those burners are weak. Once I had your number, it was an easy matter to—"

I didn't let him finish before I cracked him in the nose and walked to the computer as he stumbled backward. "Those men tried to kill me, Arthur, twice, which means either you don't have the pull you think you do"—I pulled the drive out of the computer—"or you don't give a shit about me. Either way, I'm going to have to deny your offer."

"You stupid whore. Who do you—"

This time I smashed my fist into his face. "I would leave town."

"You bitch! I—"

I cracked him again in the jaw and sent him unconscious. It felt really, really good. I hopped over him to the living room, where I found Dodo. "Come on."

He pushed up to sit. "I heard what you said. You didn't sell me out."

"Don't get too mushy about it," I replied. "If you don't get up off your ass, I'm leaving you here."

CHAPTER FIFTY-ONE

This was a stupid idea in a sea of stupid ideas, and when I pulled Dodo's Tesla up in front of the Looking Glass Lounge, all I could think was one thing: *How the fuck did my life come to this?*

I pulled Dodo out of the car and leaned down to his ear. "Are you sure you're okay with this?"

"Absolutely not, but I doubt you are, either."

"Fair enough."

I pressed my gun tightly into Dodo's temple and walked forward. It was the morning, and the bar was closed, but a lion still stood outside. "Go away."

"Tell Caterpillar I know who killed his man and who the White Queen is." I cocked the gun. "Oh, and that his favorite coder will die right here."

The lion looked at me for a long time. "I don't get paid enough for this shit."

He turned and gestured me inside. The main stage had been turned into a bed, and Caterpillar lay in it, looking comfortable as ever and dead to the world. The lion cleared his throat, and Caterpillar roused.

"What the fuck, Carmen?" he shouted. "I told you not to interrupt me when I'm—" Caterpillar looked over at me. His head was matted to his face, and he wiped the drool from it. "Oh, it's you." It took him a second to realize who I was, and then his eyes went wide. Gone were the affectations of his voice that he used when he was in control. "Wait! You're supposed to be dead!"

"And I'm not," I replied. "I prefer you better when you're not using that terrible lisp. It's really unbecoming."

"Don't change the subject!" He replied, every word harsher than the last. "I talked to Eddy. He told me you killed his partner and left him on the side of the road."

I rubbed my temples. "That's not even half—it doesn't matter. I know you want to kill me, but I need your help, and I think you're going to want my help, too."

He hopped down from the bed. "And why would I do that?"

"Because she knows who killed William and the identity of the White Queen."

Caterpillar stepped down from the stage. "And that's supposed to interest me, why?"

"Please, you're sleeping in your bar." I pulled Dodo close to me. "It's obvious you're scared of leaving this place, which is pathetic."

"I'm not scared. I could leave any time I wanted."

"Fine." I sighed. "But I can tell you who the White Queen is right now and give you evidence you can use to bring down the whole of her operation and indict half the city. All you have to do is stop trying to kill me and let me out of my contract with you."

He scratched his chin. "But I do so want to kill you."

"Trust me," Dodo said. "You're really gonna wanna hear this, and also, I'm gonna need some of that protection, too."

Caterpillar thought for a long moment, then nodded. "Very well, if you can produce evidence I can use to eviscerate the White Queen, I will call off the hit on you and let you out of your contract with me, but it had better be airtight."

"Oh," I dropped my gun into its holster and pulled out the thumb drive. "It is."

True to his word, Caterpillar called off his hit on me the minute he saw what was on the hard drive. It didn't take him long to put his massive network into action, sending the video to every news outlet in Wonderland and starting a massive shitstorm that buried Councilwoman Lane and Jack Fowler under it.

I very much enjoyed watching Mr. Deedum get arrested and dragged off in cuffs, along with his boss, who thought he was untouchable—but I touched him, and the White Queen fell that day, and Arthur fell with her, along with every member of her network. The worst part about Arthur ended up being that he really didn't like Legos after all. Oh, and that he gave Mr. Deedum the keys to my place so they could break in, even though I expressly told him not to make a copy. They were both probably equally bad.

We found out in the coming weeks that Jack Fowler recruited the Cards to deal for the White Queen and either paid people off or forced their cooperation through Black Jack Security. When something leaked to the media, it was Arthur's job to squash it as fast as possible, and he was good at his job.

It was all for the best that it didn't work out with him. I was a lone wolf, and I liked it that way.

AUTHOR NOTES

I had the seeds of this idea many years ago and even released the first 10,000 words of White Rabbit to my newsletter when I was a much younger writer. Every few months people would ask me about doing more, but it wasn't until I sped up my writing that I was able to write enough books and get enough space to write this duology.

I know it's corny to make the boyfriend an accomplice, but I always loved when people did it in the thrillers I read growing up. I usually make the boyfriend/girlfriend the helper, so it was nice to have a change of pace where one of the bad guys was sleeping with the main character. It feels like a very thriller thing to do.

And this is a thriller, through and through. I was very excited to be able to pull out of fantasy and write something that was absolutely purely a thriller. Most of my fantasy work, especially the Godsverse Chronicles, have thriller tendencies, but this was the first series I've written in a while where people couldn't just explode things at will.

It was also the first book I've written that took place in one city since all the way back in 2019, which might not feel like a long time, especially being as I wrote this at the end of 2021, But I've written 25 novels since then, which is basically like having a career in just a few short years.

I really hope you enjoyed this story and Alice. Now, we will wait for the reception to see if there will be more from Wonderland.

ALSO BY RUSSELL NOHELTY

THE OBSIDIAN SPINDLE SAGA
The Sleeping Beauty
The Wicked Witch
The Fairy Queen
The Red Rider
THE GODVERSE CHRONICLES
And Death Followed Behind Her
And Doom Followed Behind Her
And Ruin Followed Behind Her
And Hell Followed Behind Her
And Conquest Followed Behind Them
And Darkness Followed Behind Her
And Chaos Followed Behind Them
Katrina Hates the Dead
Pixie Dust
OTHER NOVEL WORK
My Father Didn't Kill Himself
Sorry for Existing
Gumshoes: The Case of Madison's Father
The Invasion Saga
The Vessel
Worst Thing in the Universe
The Void Calls Us Home
The Marked Ones
OTHER ILLUSTRATED WORK
The Little Bird and the Little Worm
Ichabod Jones: Monster Hunter
Gherkin Boy
www.russellnohelty.com